W9-DBQ-419

Poster Boy

POSTER BOY

Dede Crane

GROUNDWOOD BOOKS
HOUSE OF ANANSI PRESS
Toronto   Berkeley

Groundwood Books / House of Anansi Press
110 Spadina Avenue, Suite 801, Toronto, Ontario M5V 2K4
or c/o Publishers Group West
1700 Fourth Street, Berkeley, CA 94710

We acknowledge for their financial support of our publishing program the Canada
Council for the Arts, the Government of Canada through the Book Publishing
Industry Development Program (BPIDP) and the Ontario Arts Council.

Library and Archives Canada Cataloguing in Publication
Crane, Dede
Poster boy / Dede Crane.
ISBN 978-0-88899-855-2 (bound).–ISBN 978-0-88899-861-3 (pbk.)
I. Title.
PS8605.R35P68 2009   jC813'.6   C2009-901070-4

Cover illustration by Gary Sawyer
Design by Michael Solomon
Printed and bound in Canada

For Vaughn

1 The Friends

"Chuck Norris doesn't read books. He stares them down until he gets the information he needs."

It was Friday night at my house. My best bud, Davis, trying to recall old Chuck Norris jokes. Five of us were in the hot tub, others inside on the computer or playing Xbox. I had dope rock on the stereo, one speaker set just outside the door of my "sweet."

Nine months ago, my mom moved her silkscreen stuff out of the basement and into the pimped-up shed out back, and I moved down from my room upstairs. Tonight my parents were home, but they were chill as long as we didn't trash the place or piss off the neighbors.

"Chuck Norris doesn't sleep. He waits." Davis laughed, and we laughed at his pathetically dumb laugh. Taking great gulps of air, he snorted and hiccuped like some drunk hillbilly.

"Lame, Davis," said Natalie. Erin, her sidekick, nodded.

"You're lame," said Hughie as he splashed her.

Whipping her face away, Nat's breast pressed against

my arm, her bare thigh against my leg. I had to remind myself to breathe.

Natalie was ringleader of the popular girls at school. My friends and I were fringe stoner types. Three weeks ago at the Halloween dance, she touched me on the shoulder and asked me to dance.

"You know who you remind me of?" she said. I just shook my head. "Johnny Depp in that Scissorhands movie."

I was dressed as a vampire, my brown hair gob-slicked with gel. I was naturally thin, pale, had the sunken-cheek thing going on, and Mom had done my eyes with black eyeliner. I made a sick vampire.

Natalie, though, was majorly hot. Silky black hair, cat-shaped eyes, caramel skin, body like Scarlett Johansson. Her voice was more like Lois's on *Family Guy* and drove Davis crazy but didn't distract me. She dressed to enhance, wore blue mascara and regularly applied a tiny wand to her lips which smelled of coconut. To kiss her tasted like wax but who cared.

I'd just turned sixteen. Still had my V-card. Was primed for love.

Ciel came out with the ice cubes that Natalie had asked for. Ciel (pronounced See-el, as in French for sky) had just moved from city to burbs and into the house across from Natalie's. Nat's mom had insisted she invite her along tonight. Ciel was in our grade but seemed older – read duller.

"Ice?" she asked flatly. Standing over the hot tub, she

began to twist them out of the tray. They dropped like rocks into the water, and we scrambled to catch them. I caught two and slipped one down Natalie's top.

"Ahh... stop," she yelled, standing up to slap my head, her breasts at eye level. "You asked for it." She slipped hers down the front of my shorts, incidentally brushing the self. Under the camouflage of bubbles, the self saluted.

Trying to be casual, I threw back my head and laughed.

Davis and I had been calling our dongs the self ever since grade two when we had a kid in our class named Deeki. A super happy-looking kid, Deeki had a habit of storing one hand inside his pants. Deeki enjoyed holding onto his dickie. Our teacher, Mrs. Sweeney, used to say to him in slow-moron English, "We do not touch our *self* in school." As she stressed the word, her prim eyes glanced off Deeki's crotch to aid her point.

It all made perfect sense to me and Davis. Our self was our dick and our dick our self.

Davis was now balancing three ice cubes on his blond head and whistling the national anthem. Thankfully, the self was calming down.

Davis and I had known each other since we were snot-nosed kindergartners fidgeting on our squares of colored carpet. Terminally bored, Davis spent most of his kinder-garten day making faces or farts to get the other kids to laugh. I was the kid that laughed the loudest, and we did a lot of bonding from our respective time-out corners.

"Why don't you come in, Ciel?" said Erin, glancing at Natalie.

"Don't feel like getting wet." Ciel was the only person not in a bathing suit.

"When Chuck Norris gets in a hot tub, he doesn't get wet. The water gets Chuck Norrised," said Davis, horking laughter, ice cubes sliding off his head. He caught one, threw it in the air and caught it again in his mouth.

"Anyone for ping-pong?" asked Ciel. She looked around the circle for takers and her eyes landed on mine. If eyes could sneer, hers were sneering. I looked away.

"I'll play," said Davis. In one smooth move, he hopped over the side of the tub and onto the deck.

Davis was unnaturally coordinated. Short and stubby (my polar opposite) he was always the best player on any sports team. Until, that is, he got kicked off for not showing up. I think it was his not caring that made him so good. He never choked because he never cared if he choked.

"Davis powns nubes," Hughie warned Ciel.

"Pardon me?" she asked, the eye sneer infecting her whole face.

"Powns means owns and nubes are newbies like you," said Hughie.

"Meaning he's impossible to beat," I translated. Even when stoned and drunk, Davis would beat you at ping-pong.

"I'm up for a challenge," said Ciel, sounding bored. I couldn't help thinking that the girl with the pretentious name was one stuck-up bitch.

I slipped my hand around Natalie's bare waist and she didn't flinch. Her slippery softness made my head swoon, and I had to sit up on the edge of the tub.

"Be merciful," Hughie called as Davis and Ciel went inside.

"Anyone see *Survivor* last night?" asked Natalie, nuzzling her shoulder against my knobby knee. "That new guy's scary."

"Yeah," echoed Erin.

"But he has such a cool hair cut," continued Natalie. "Shaved on the sides and long on top. That would look good on you, Gray."

Clean-cut was the new hip. Davis and I were the only two of our friends who still had long hair.

Natalie kept talking but I barely noticed what came out of her mouth, because from my lofty angle I couldn't get past what was coming out of her bathing suit top.

The others started to get out and go inside. When Natalie started out, I stopped her with a kiss. Her lips were two chubby velvet cushions. Unlike me, she was a confident kisser. She had a make-out routine that I did my best to follow – a few times around my tongue, a slide along my top teeth, some deep-throat challenge, then a slide across my lower teeth, one last trip around the tongue and a smacking kiss to separate. I liked the teeth thing a lot.

But tonight, afraid she might be thinking I was some kind of wuss, it was time to go beyond kissing. Earlier I'd had a couple of confidence-boosting shots of the vodka Davis had scored off one of his half-brothers.

Sitting on the tub's edge, our bodies steaming in the fall air, I did a quick check for my spying sneak of a little sister. No sign of her. I kissed Nat's neck, one eye straining to watch my hand as it tentatively cupped her left breast. When she didn't say anything, I touched more firmly, my nerves doing a crazy-ass dance.

I waited for a reaction. Nothing. Did that mean she liked it? Or maybe it needed to be skin on skin for the girl to get off. She was probably waiting for just that and thinking I was a douche. Hoping my hand wasn't shaking, I slipped it inside her suit… couldn't breathe and had to stop the neck-kissing part before I passed out.

Natalie still wasn't doing anything. It wasn't like her to be this quiet.

Hand still holding the goods, I looked at her.

"Do you… uh…" – it was hard to get enough air – "Want to… go back… inside?"

"Sure," she said, all bubbly.

Oh. I slipped out my hand.

Natalie's smile was so white it seemed to glow in the dark. She readjusted her top.

"*Next Top Model*'s on tonight," she said. "You got to see the legs on this one girl."

* * *

Inside, Ciel was losing to Davis but not by much.

"I'm kicking her newbie ass but she won't give up," said Davis when he saw me.

Natalie wandered over to Chrissy and Erin on the computer. Hughie and Parmjot were playing Xbox. Watching the ping-pong ball click back and forth, I tried to figure out what I did wrong out there. Was there some trick, some technique I should know about?

Ciel missed Davis's serve and grunted at herself. Seemed to be taking the game seriously and was going to be pissed, I thought, when she lost.

"Parm, do you spell your name like the cheese?" Natalie asked.

Not missing a shot, Davis laughed. "Yeah, Parmesan. Mom name you after her favorite cheese?"

"That right," Parmjot laughed.

The girls looked confused. Obviously they'd discussed this question before.

"Just kidding," Parmjot assured them.

"It's Parmjot, you idiots," said Hughie. "Not jan."

"Don't call us – "

"Means stinky cheese in Punjabi," laughed Davis as he gave the ball an overhand spin and it blew by Ciel.

"Come on," she reprimanded herself and retrieved the ball to serve for game point. Davis's, that is, which he effortlessly won.

I was surprised to see her laugh when she lost.

"You make it look so easy." She looked admiringly at Davis. I suddenly wanted her to look at me that way.

"Just a stupid game," Davis shrugged.

I grabbed a paddle and began juggling the ball. "You want a chance to redeem your – "

"Gray," called Natalie. "Where's the remote? You guys have to stop that stupid game. *Top Model*'s on. This one girl has legs like a giraffe."

I found the remote and Natalie pulled me down beside

her to watch these freakishly tall skinny girls with their freakishly tall skinny legs bitch at each other.

I saw a flash of movement to my left and realized my twelve-year-old sister, Maggie, and her friend Sasha were eavesdropping on the stairs. Maggie was always spying and trying to get something on me.

"It's red and a convertible!" Erin was inheriting her grandmother's old Beemer.

"I love Beemers," cooed Chrissy.

"Hey, Hughie." I mouthed the word "Maggie" and indicated with my head.

Hughie's eyes lit up and he casually backed up toward the stairs. Then, in one fluid, well-practiced motion, he bent over while yanking down his jeans. Maggie and her friend laugh-screamed and ran upstairs.

"Put that frightening thing away," said Natalie.

"Really," echoed Erin.

"Was that Maggie?" asked Chrissy. "She's so cute."

"Maggots are not cute," I said.

Davis pulled his bong from his backpack. It was time for the guys to go blaze in the bathroom with the fan on. Us guys would get wrecked and speechless, while the girls sipped their orange pop and vodka and predicted America's Next Top Bitch.

I looked at this Ciel girl flipping through one of my music mags and wondered what she'd do. Her clothes didn't give anything away. Her tight turquoise jeans were cool enough, but the white blouse was major conservative, as were her white sneakers.

As if she sensed she was being watched, she honed in on me with those critical eyes. I turned back to the TV.

"Maggie would look so good with her hair short. Like that redhead, see?" Natalie pointed at the screen. "With the feathered bangs."

"Yeah, really," agreed Erin.

"You, too, Ciel. With your eyes, you could definitely do short."

Ciel kept on reading.

"You want to cut everybody's hair off," said Hughie. "You're like a serial hair killer."

Davis laughed and we laughed at him laughing until Natalie shushed us. "Shut up, I want to hear this."

Ciel, surprisingly, blazed with us guys. She had one hit while the rest of us had two. The stuff was pretty strong, and after about ten minutes I realized one hit would have been plenty.

Huey, Parm and Davis went outside to the tub, but Natalie's half-naked body beckoned me to the couch. My hand rubbing her shoulder, I made wishes on her golden skin while on TV, someone named Miss Jay ran around in a nurse's costume. She had this deep voice and was sincerely ugly. Was she a he? Then these skinny girls were naked except for straitjackets and Natalie, in high-whine commentary, was saying something about one of the girls being autistic.

I was trying to figure out why autistic people would have to wear straitjackets when I stopped hearing the TV and noticed this super sad tune coming out of my guitar.

Ciel was sitting in the far corner on the floor. The turquoise of her pants seemed to pulse against the neon-yellow walls behind her, and I was tempted to get my camera. A curtain of brown hair covered her face, and her slender body curved around my guitar.

The sounds coming from that guitar were suddenly the only sounds in the room that made any sense. That is until I heard Davis laughing outside.

And then I started to laugh, though I didn't even know what was funny.

2   The Family

I was dragged out of sleep by the sound of people arguing. Then I remembered it was Saturday. The Russian roulette team was here.

Since she was getting more silkscreen jobs, Mom had hired, at a neighbor's recommendation, Sergei and Dasha to help with the housework. They were Russian dissidents – asylum seekers, we were told, crimes against the government. I imagined they were spies. The kind that could kill you in seconds with a matchstick or a spoon.

Sergei did the heavier work like the sweeping and mopping, and moving the furniture to vacuum, while Dasha sprayed things. She loved her aerosols, wore them like pistols in a tool belt around her waist. He had a scar across the bridge of his off-centered nose, a buzz cut and a wiry but muscular build. She had big hair with bangs that trailed into black eyes that looked passionately depressed.

They both scared the shit out of me.

The vacuum growled into gear and I checked the clock. Noon. Mom had probably sent them down here just to wake me up. She wouldn't allow them to clean the bathrooms – "too demeaning" – which meant I'd have to clean mine today. And yes, it was demeaning.

I slipped on some clothes and opened the door, my hair blown back by a bomb of ammonia and Lemon Pledge. Dasha was on her knees crop-dusting the coffee table.

"Morning." I raised a nervous hand.

Dasha lifted her sad eyes to me and Sergei shot me a dark look.

I escaped into the bathroom, locking the door behind me.

*   *   *

Upstairs, Mom, Dad and Maggie were in the kitchen. Mom ironing fabric, Dad and Maggie at the table hunched over some book. The brightness of the room hurt my eyes. The kitchen walls were the color of tangerines, the counters turquoise, the cupboards white with yellow trim. Mom had silkscreened curtains that, according to her, blended these sketchy colors together.

Mom was into color, claimed it stimulated brain-cell growth, though Dad said that study was directed to infants. A new cell was an infant, Mom said. Whatever, Maggie's bedroom was praying-mantis green, Mom and Dad's firecracker red. The living and dining room were bronze with royal blue curtains. The rec room downstairs a painfully cheery yellow. There wasn't one room in the house that didn't stimulate.

My old bedroom upstairs was bright purple. When I moved downstairs, Mom said I could choose the color for my new bedroom. I chose black. Mom changed her mind.

We compromised on one black wall, the other three a blue-gray covered with black-and-white posters of my fave bands. With the sharp end of a compass, I'd etched the words of "Californication" into the black wall. My room rocked.

"This picture's amazing," said Maggie, squinting over her book.

"You just getting up?" Dad asked. I grunted in the affirmative.

"There's batter in the fridge," said Mom. "I left the waffle iron out. Just plug it in. And have a nectarine."

I plugged in the waffle iron. "Stink."

"Nail polish," said Mom, sliding open the deck door.

"I painted the nails on Dad's new girl hand," said Maggie, picking it up and thrusting it in my direction. "Need a hand with those waffles?"

Dad was a bio-mechanic up at the university. Prosthetics. Made myoelectric hands. A creepy way to make a living, but somebody had to do it. We had a lot of bad hand jokes in our family.

Maggie scratched her head with the nails of the rubber hand.

"Dad thinks I should do my science project on how negative and positive intention influences the vibrational level of matter."

I had no clue what my sister the geek had just said. I was allergic to science fairs and glad as hell those days were behind me. Dad, Mr. Myoelectric, used to be keen to help with my projects, too. He'd come up with something using hot wires and electric currents – things that could kill you if you touched the wrong ends. As he did the bulk of my project, I would stand real close as if I was doing it, too. He'd explain stuff and I'd not understand it but write it down word for word. I'd get a blue ribbon and feel like a guilty-ass cheater.

"This Japanese scientist, Dr. Emoto," explained Dad, "has experimented with exposing water to various stimuli and taking microscopic photos of the crystals that form when that water's frozen. It's really pretty fascinating."

I caught Mom's eye and she smiled.

"I bet you didn't know trees are eighty percent water?" said Maggie.

"Did," I lied.

Like Dad, Maggie went gaga over the factual world – why bees swarmed, why leaves changed color, how tiny worms set up house at the base of each eyelash, Guinness world records.

Like Mom, I preferred the abstract. She'd gone the art college route. Used to be into drawing and painting, but when I was maybe two, she got turned onto silkscreen – a method of printing ink designs on fabric. She started off selling scarves and stuff at craft fairs, later to boutiques. But in August she scored her first big commission: a dozen silkscreen banners for the new bank coming to Jackson Street in the spring. Danced around the house for a week.

My thing was photography, though I didn't know if I was any good. I went roaming with Davis, took pictures of whatever caught my eye. Clouds were cool, doorknobs, close-ups of rusted things, and trees at night. But then, smoking a little weed made everything look cool.

"He's exposed water to Beatles music, Beethoven, Elvis, acid rock," continued Dad. "You should really see some of these photos, Gray."

Later, I thought, not responding. Not responding was often simplest.

"The acid rock photos didn't form any crystals at all," said Maggie. "They're just these blobs."

"What are you up to today, Gray?" asked Mom.

"Stuff."

"What time do you work?"

"Five." I worked Wednesdays and Saturdays at the Cineplex. Selling tickets, filling bottomless buckets of popcorn and Coke, sweeping candy wrappers off the floor. The job was a job but I got to preview movies, invite a friend. I was saving for some beater van, seventies style, mattress in the back. Wanted a car you could travel in.

Only problem was I always needed stuff – clothes, shoes or delish foot-longs from Safeway – so hadn't saved more than a few hundred.

"Need a ride?" asked Mom.

"Sure."

"You can practice driving."

I grunted. I'd just got my Learners.

"Take a vitamin C with your breakfast. Maggie's coming down with a cold."

"My leg aches." Maggie rolled her eyes. "You don't get a cold in one leg."

"Just to be safe."

Mom was an involved parent. Had the maternal instincts of a moose, claimed Dad. Mother moose, according to him, were the most deadly animals on the planet.

Mom turned to me. "How was the party?"

"Fine." I was concentrating on filling all the squares of the waffle iron with just the right amount of batter, otherwise it spilled over when you closed the top.

"Don't forget you have to do your bathroom before you go anywhere."

"Yeah."

"My son speaks in single word sentences," sighed Dad.

"Chimpanzees can give single word responses," said Maggie.

"My point exactly."

"He's sixteen," said Mom.

"You'd think he'd have learned to speak by now," said Dad.

"Just remember when you were sixteen," said Mom.

"I was a nerd, remember?"

"Was?" I said.

Dad and Mom both laughed and I couldn't help smiling. For some reason it feels dope to make your parents laugh.

"Good one, Gray," said Dad. "A single word with some punch. Nerds made your precious computer and Xbox, don't forget."

"Cool nerds," I said.

"Ooh, two words together," said Dad. "He gets a banana."

"I don't know why people think being dumb is cool," said Maggie. "Like what Hughie did last night."

"What did Hughie do last night?" asked Mom.

"Nothing," I said, meeting Maggie's eye.

"Nothing," said Maggie and gave me a you-owe-me smile.

Mom asked Dad what he thought of her fabric choice. He said something nice and she kissed his head.

When I compared my parents to my friends' parents, who criped and yapped at each other, had affairs or drank too much, half of them separated or divorced, I might say they got on famously. Davis, for example, had a total of three moms and two dads. Go figure. But according to him none of them got on any better than the last. His various parents would fight even in front of guests, namely me. And with their kids.

I once saw his dad slap Davis across the face for some "smart ass" remark – though I think Davis was sincerely trying to be funny. It was a hard hit, too. Davis's cheek was red for the rest of the day. Though it could have been from embarrassment. It's shitty enough to get face-slapped but a whole lot shittier in front of a friend. Davis didn't tell a joke for a week.

"Mag," said Mom, "I'm going to have some leftover fabric. You could silkscreen some scarves. Would make nice Christmas gifts for your teachers?"

"I have only one female teacher," corrected Maggie.

"Ties, then?"

"Sure."

If it wasn't for the scary cleaning people, I would have taken my waffles downstairs to eat at the computer. Instead I was forced to sit at the kitchen table and look at a photo of a six-sided water crystal formed after being exposed to Elvis singing "Heartbreak Hotel." It actually looked like two crystals mushed together.

"The crystal's broken apart," said Maggie, awed.

"I'll be damned," said Dad.

3   Girlfriends

Trig class. I was on top of it at the beginning of the year, sort of, but in the past few weeks I'd gone into a kind of coma.

The bell rang. I looked at the assignment on the board, then at my notes. There on the page were detailed drawings of sushi.

Trig was the last class before lunch. I looked back at the board.

I couldn't ask Hughie to decipher the assignment because I'd heard him snoring behind me during class. Then I noticed that Ciel chick copying down the homework as if she understood it. I went over to her desk.

"Hey, Ciel. How's it going?"

She kept writing.

"It's Gray, remember me from – "

"I do." She didn't sound thrilled by the memory.

"Great shirt," I said before I noticed how plain it was. A black T-shirt.

She gathered her books to leave.

"Do you actually understand this stuff?"

"I do." She razored me with those eyes of hers. Brown, I noted, with copper rings around the pupil.

"I kind of get it, but missed a few things today." I put on my hangdog face. "Would you mind, horribly, explaining it to me over lunch?"

"Me, too?" said Hughie suddenly beside me, his hair all sleep-wrecked.

"If you buy me a Caramilk bar from the vending machine." She smiled. A greedy sort of smile.

"Yeah, sure."

She looked at Hughie. "Two."

"Oh. Okay," agreed Hughie.

She went on ahead and we followed like sheep.

"Two what?" whispered Hughie.

We had a "study-lunch" with Ciel once a week after that. The rest of the week's lunchtimes, I either played soccer Frisbee with the guys or hung with Natalie and her friends.

Ciel and Natalie had gone their separate ways. Ciel now hung with the band types and the environmental club – the Turn-Off-Your-Lights-to-Save-the-Marmot Club as Davis called it.

Lucky for Hughie and me, Ciel was Maggie-smart. Not a lot of humor going on, but she had a very clear way of explaining things. She didn't linger, didn't take questions, and never ate her Caramilks in front of us. I imagined them stacked under her bed like gold bars.

Just before Christmas break we had a major quiz worth twenty percent of our mark, so I invited her to my house to "study" with me and Hughie. Sounded less desperate than "teach us everything now." Our books spread out on the floor of my sweet, she summarized trig facts as if it was idiot proof and then tried, not very successfully, to hide her impatience when we needed stuff repeated.

But I found studying her more interesting. The way she held her head so erect I wanted to balance a book on it. And how her brown hair had these hidden gold strands when the light hit it, and the slight hollows under her cheekbones held tiny shadows. As she explained the differences between sine, cosine and tangent, I thought how Natalie's body curved like hill and valley while Ciel's was like water flowing gently downhill. How Natalie's body was pop music and Ciel was that lyrical jazz stuff Dad listened...

"Gray?"

"Huh?" I removed my eyes from her butt.

"Are you with us?" asked Ciel.

"I'm getting it," I nodded. She looked doubtful. "Go on," I said.

I watched the intensity in her face as she wrote out the equation "the ratio of the side opposite a given angle to the hypotenuse" like a magnifying glass focusing sunlight. I imagined a brown spot appearing on the white page of the textbook, then a searing hole, the brown edges spreading outward, the book bursting into...

"So what would you use to solve this problem? Sine or cos?" Ciel looked directly at me, blinding me with her Super Sight.

"It's Hughie's turn to answer," I said, looking at Hughie.

"What?" said Hughie.

"Come on, man, pay attention," I said. "One more time for Hughie here." I shook my head apologetically.

She sighed. "Do you guys really want to pass this class?"

"Yes," we said in chorus, because to have to take trig all over again next semester would be self abuse.

And not the good kind.

Hughie took his Caramilk bar from his jacket pocket. "Want this now?"

"No," she said and started from the top.

* * *

Thanks to Ciel, I passed the quiz. Hughie, too. Not by much, but we passed. The next day was the Christmas Red and Green dance. Boo yeah. Dances at our school kicked ass. I'd bought a red shirt at American Eagle, stuffed a little pine branch in my pocket, sprinkled gold glitter in my hair.

The night of the dance, Davis got a friend of his brother's to buy us some beer which he, Hughie and I drank behind the baseball bleachers beforehand. The ground was all crunchy, our breath cartoon clouds.

Hughie wore a green tunic and tights like Will Ferrell in *Elf.* He had a spliff taped behind the red feather in his green cap.

"This stuff is dank," said Hughie, lighting up.

"I got some seeds from my half-sister's boyfriend's brother," said Davis. "I'm going to grow me some blazing, ripping, danking, Mary Jane-me-up-the-ass weed."

"Have you ever grown anything?" I laughed.

"My dick."

God, I loved Davis.

We all took one good hit. Then Hughie snuffed it and re-taped it inside his feather.

It was a nice high, all sparkly like the December night. It gave me a feeling of belonging to something bigger than myself, and I could actually relax a little. Or maybe that was the beer part. There were some cool ragged clouds wrapped around a half moon. The more I looked at it, the more I could swear it made the perfect profile of our science teacher, Mr. Sneddon.

I nudged Davis and pointed. "Mr. Sneddon."

He looked up and laughed.

"Yeah, yeah," he said, and I was sure he understood.

"If only I had my camera."

"Yeah," said Davis, and we walked toward the gym.

I was feeling fine as I headed inside to meet Natalie. Saw her in the ticket line with Erin. Skin tight and satiny, her dress was Christmas-ball red and man, did it stimulate. It hung off one shoulder, toga style, and was cut low in the front. A mini cheering section in my head chanted, CLEA-VAGE... CLEA-VAGE... CLEA-VAGE.

When she saw me looking, she did a little turn on her black heels.

"You like?"

"Wow!" I tried to lift my eyes from her chest to her face but they moved at mud speed.

"She made it herself," said Erin. "In Sewing."

"Yeah," I said. In that moment I felt totally in love, not only with Nat but with kowtowing Erin and the ticket sellers, the frowning principal, Ms. Jackson, standing behind them – even the macho jocks laughing down the hall.

"Let's see what you're wearing," demanded Nat, and I obediently took off my jacket.

She turned up the collar of my shirt. "You look good in red, Gray Fallon."

"You…" was all I managed.

"American Eagle… nice. And I like the shoes."

I'd also bought a new pair of off-white skate shoes.

And then, feeling like I'd passed some final test, she slipped her arm in mine, leaned her beautiful head on my shoulder and provided me a direct view down the cleave tunnel.

The DJ was excellent, playing a good range of stuff and not just all techno. A highlight of the evening was getting further acquainted with Natalie's breasts in the equipment room. As long as I didn't mess up her hair or make-up, she didn't seem to mind.

It amazed me that her chest was so radically different from my own. Ridiculously soft, those two things. Quiet, too, unlike Natalie who, between kisses, kept talking about Erin liking some tenth grader named Erin, too, only spelled Aaron.

"That'll be so weird if they go out. Or got married. Wouldn't that be too funny?"

As the dance wound down, I thought to look for Ciel, thank her for the miracle of me and Hughie passing that quiz. It was a strategy move, since I'd need her help even more come final exams.

I asked Natalie if she'd seen her.

"She didn't come. Had some concert thing." She rolled her eyes.

I was supposed to work at the theater but had called in sick.

"What sort of concert?" I asked, picturing Ciel playing my guitar.

"My mom's like in love with Ciel," Natalie went on. "Thinks she's the perfect child. I hate that when your parents think somebody else's kid is so great. It's like they want to trade you in."

"I mean what instrument does she play?"

"The harp." Nat made a face. "Who plays the harp?"

"Angels?" I said, as Erin and Chrissy rushed over all frantic and pulled Natalie away to share some gossipy secret.

Walking home that night, the dope and beer now a dimmed buzz, I felt stupid content. Like my life was one long smooth road. No bumps, no curves, not even a stop light.

4 The Phone Call

It was a couple weeks after Christmas break. I'd just come home from school and was in the kitchen grabbing a snack — two frozen mini-pizzas, a half-dozen cookies, a pound of milk. Mom was at the table examining some fabric she'd just dyed part "lantern orange" and part "tobacco gold."

Maggie came into the kitchen limping.

"Hi, sweetheart," said Mom. "How was your day?"

"What's wrong with you?" I snorted.

"My leg's really sore, okay?" she snapped.

"Wimp," I added, and she slugged me.

"Ow." She was surprisingly strong for a wimp.

"What did you do in gym today?" asked Mom, putting down her fabric.

I put the pizzas in the microwave to nuke for three minutes.

"We don't have gym on Tuesdays," said Maggie. She climbed onto a stool with a groan.

"Maybe it's from skiing?" I said.

Over break our family had gone skiing for the first time ever, meaning snowboarding. I got the knack right away.

Being a throbhead with no natural rhythm, Maggie couldn't snowboard to save her life. She'd taken some pretty bad falls but never complained. Just got out there and beat herself up the next day, too. I'm not sure her brain knew she had a body.

"That was weeks ago," she said.

"Maybe it's taken this long for the pain to register."

Maggie lifted her foot onto the other stool and examined her calf.

"I don't see a bruise," she said to Mom, "but there's a bump. Here, feel."

"We should go skiing over March break." I'd found out that Nat was going up with Erin's family.

Mom felt Maggie's leg. "A ganglian cyst, most likely, Magpie. They're harmless."

"Ganglian," Maggie repeated.

"If you purchase a lift ticket before February first you save twenty percent." I'd been doing research.

"We'll see, Gray." She turned back to Maggie. "I had a ganglian cyst on the web between my thumb and forefinger once and it went away on its own after a few months." She patted Maggie's leg.

"We could stay at the – "

"My doctor at the time," laughed Mom, "told me there's a tradition of taking Bibles to these cysts. Thumping the bump, he called it. Supposed to work."

"Shall I get the hammer?" I said.

"Get away from me," said Maggie.

"Get your sister the ice pack, please, Gray?" said Mom.

"If you say we'll go skiing."

She gave me her exasperated look. "Don't push it, Gray. Now, Maggie, go put your feet up and ice your leg for ten. It'll be fine."

"Catch." I tossed the ice pack across the kitchen. Maggie wasn't ready for it and it smacked her on the shoulder.

"Ow! Thanks a lot, Graydumb." My full name was Graydon.

"Gotta work on those reflexes." The microwave beeped.

She picked the ice pack up off the floor. "Oh, my back hurts, too."

Mom put her lips to Maggie's forehead, then lifted her hair to do the same to the back of her neck.

"Are you drinking enough water? Go put your feet up and I'll bring you a – "

"But I need to cook rice for my science project," huffed Maggie. "And sterilize three jars. I have to take observations for ten weeks."

Maggie had decided on the water project. But because she didn't have the conditions to study ice crystals, she was doing her experiment using cooked rice, which contained water. This was also in the Japanese guy's book. You put the rice in three different jars. One jar you ignored, one you said nice things to and one you yelled at. Then you observed what happened to each over several weeks.

It sounded hokey to me but, hey, it wasn't my project. Thank God.

"How do you cook rice?" Maggie was brainy at brainy things and a retard for ordinary everyday stuff.

"Read the package, why don't you?" I escaped down-stairs with my food to pound some music and see if Nat was online.

* * *

A week later, Maggie and I were making our lunches for school. She kept harping on about her right arm being asleep.

"It's been almost an hour and it won't wake up," she whined. "It's all tingly and numb."

I leaned over and put my face next to her arm.

"Wake up!" I yelled, and she elbowed me in the face. I grabbed her arm and twisted it behind her back.

"Is it awake now?"

She gasped and, instinctively, I let go. Tears sprang to her eyes as she grabbed her forearm.

Maggie never cried when I tortured her.

"You *are* turning into a wimp."

She didn't smile, didn't hit me, just took deep breaths.

"Sorry," I said, because I guess I actually hurt her. "You okay?"

She nodded and winced at the same time.

When I told Mom about it later, she lowered her voice and said, "I think your sister's about to get her period."

Oh, gawd. Too much information.

"Don't look like that, Gray," she said to my retreating back. "It's part of the cycle of life and something to cele-brate. I'm planning to take her downtown for lunch when it…"

I plugged my ears and hummed the national anthem.

* * *

By Sunday, Maggie's arm still hadn't woken up. The pain in her calf was back along with the limp. Her back still ached whenever she bent over, yet she showed no signs of a cold or flu or the big exclamation mark.

Dad thought she should be checked out. Being Sunday, he took her to a drop-in clinic. The doctor said there was a virus going around that affected the limbs and not to worry. He sent her home with some Tylenol.

Sunday nights we watched *Lost* together. It was the one show we all got into. Dad claimed the Lay-Z-boy, as always, and Maggie got my spot on the couch so Mom could massage her feet, which meant I got Maggie's uncomfortable beanbag chair.

Watching Maggie's foot in Mom's hands, I was jealous as hell. I couldn't remember the last time she'd given me one. Mom's foot massages felt unbelievably dope. I was starting to think Maggie was probably faking.

"It might be growing pains, Magpie," said Dad during a commercial – some cool car with a TV in it, speaker-phone and built-in iPod.

"Gray," said Mom, "do you remember having growing pains when you were little? You'd have trouble getting to sleep. I'd rub your legs and – "

"In my knees." I remembered how they ached and kind of burned.

"It's a question of mineralization," explained Dad. "The bones are growing faster than the body can nourish them."

"Dad would make you warm milk," said Mom.

"With honey and butter." I remembered loving the taste of that milk but that it didn't seem to help.

"And you'd sleep with ice packs under your knees."

"Ice doesn't sound good but warm milk does," said Maggie.

"Can't hurt," said Dad.

"Gray, pop a mug of milk in the micro," Mom said.

"But the show's going to — "

"Gray, just takes a minute," said Dad with that tone that instantly made me feel like a jerk.

"Honey but no butter, Gray," said Maggie. "And a pinch of cinnamon."

"Faker," I whispered, getting up.

"Am not," she hissed.

"You better be really sick." I gave her a whap on the head.

* * *

Humans, like rats, Dad often said, could adapt to anything. The pins-and-needles feeling in Maggie's arm didn't go away, but she stopped talking about it. I watched her squat to pick things up. She sat whenever there was a chair nearby. Still limped a bit, though.

Mom watched and waited for the red-letter day. Dad made lame jokes about fitting her out with fake limbs and bought Maggie's favorite ice cream — cherry jubilee, which I couldn't stand — "for the calcium and general cheering power."

Basically, I ignored her. Besides, I was busy studying for exams (with snooty girl's help), working at the Cineplex, hanging with my buds and Natalie's breasts, taking dope photos, gaming, hanging with my buds and Natalie's breasts…

I was, in short, on top of my game.

* * *

Having finished my last exam, namely trig, boo yeah, followed by a celebratory platter of nachos, I was in my sweet, music shaking the walls, logging on to MSN to see who wanted to partay the next night. I didn't ace the exam or anything, but thanks to one jumbo-sized Caramilk bar, I was sure I'd passed. Parm wrote back that he was in and was going to try and get Chrissy to come.

got the hots 4 her, do ya?

pilot light's lit.

Natalie came on line.

turning sweet sixteen and never been…

My entire body flushed with heat. Did she mean what I think she meant? I was about to write back, "me, too," but then thought that sounded unmasculine.

i'm urs. I wrote instead.

my parents r going out of town in a few weeks. we'd have the house 2 ourselves to…celebrate.

I fell back in my chair, covered my crotch with both hands and just stared at the screen for a minute, then wrote, let's hook up.

She sent me a smiley face.

I laughed out loud.

"We're going in, self ol' buddy."

Mind racing, I tried to recall pertinent sex info I'd picked up over the years. Namely from *South Park* and

Family Guy. I knew the clitoris was super important. Finding it, for starters. I mean, I wanted it to be a decent first experience for her, too. I knew it was going to rock for me no matter what, and I hated to think that twenty years from now she'd be talking about her first time as some lame joke. And birth control was important. Like I'd have to get a condom somewhere. Two. In case the first one broke. Was buying condoms like buying cigarettes and you had to be nineteen? Did they come in sizes? If so, how did you know what size you were?

how about i take u out 2 dinner first. I thought I should be a little romantic about this and not just horny.

really? that's so sweet.

Good move.

u pick the place. someplace nice.

The phone rang. Probably wasn't for me but Mom was in her studio working. She purposely didn't have a phone out there. Dad was out of town for some prosthetic conference. Maggie, I knew, was in the kitchen working on her science project. Like any good science nerd, she tuned out all distractions.

I turned down my music.

"Hello?"

"May I speak to Mr. or Mrs. Fallon, please."

"This is Mr. Fallon," I said, deepening my voice. Anyway, I wasn't lying. My English teacher regularly called me Mr. Fallon.

talk later, I typed to Nat, who was signing off. love ya, I added, just because. I'd never ever said that to a girl before.

"This is Dr. Astley's office. I'm calling with the results of Maggie's X-rays."

Just to be safe, Mom had taken Maggie to our family doctor, who'd ordered an X-ray of her sore leg.

"Uh, yes?" Mr. Fallon here is losing his V-card in a few weeks, I wanted to tell her. Got any helpful tips?

"Your daughter's X-rays have come back positive with signs of rhabdomyosarcoma."

What the... I grabbed a pen, rummaged for a scrap of paper.

"Dr. Astley wants Maggie to see an oncologist who can order further testing." The woman spoke in a steady, driving voice that didn't leave room for questions. I didn't understand what she was saying, yet my mouth had gone dry. "It'll be with Dr. Michael Bender, 1528 6th Avenue near Prince Street, tomorrow at 9:45 in the morning."

"Tomorrow?"

"Yes. 9:45. 1528 6th Avenue, which is near Prince."

She gave a tiny pause as if I might have more questions.

"There's amazing advances in therapies these days," she blurted into the gap. She sounded nervous. "I'm sorry," she added, and now I was nervous.

She was about to hang up when I stopped her.

"Can you spell that big word beginning with R?"

She spelled it.

I wanted to confess that I wasn't Maggie's father when she said good-bye and hung up.

I put down the phone, went on the net and typed in rhabdomyosarcoma.

5   Black Mold

Maggie was sitting at the kitchen table staring at her rice and carefully taking notes. Though I'd eaten a giant plate of cheese-slathered nachos with sour cream and salsa, my stomach felt weirdly hollow.

"Hey," I said.

It was like I was seeing her for the first time. She looked young for twelve and, unlike some of her friends, still undeveloped. Needless to say, Mom had yet to have her little celebration. Maggie was lanky like me. Too gawky to be pretty, she had a cute thing going on with her round face and eyes.

Sitting there all erect posture and intense focus, she reminded me of Ciel.

"Wanna see something cool?" she said, waving me over.

"Okay." I was hit with a rush of love for my little sister. But it may have been fear. I noticed she was writing with her left hand.

"Since when are you left-handed?"

"My right hand's really sore." She shook out her right hand as if, in thinking about it, she suddenly realized it hurt. "I bet my writing's already better than yours." She held up her notes.

"Yeah, it is," I said.

"Yeah, it is," she repeated and if I didn't know what I knew, I would have slapped her.

"Look at my rice."

A month ago, she'd put her cooked rice in three different jars. On one jar she pasted the word LOVE in hot-pink letters, on another the word HATE in black letters. The third jar had nothing on it. Each day she said kind words to the Love jar, verbally abused the Hate jar and deliberately ignored the third jar.

"See the mold spot in the Hate jar?"

I saw one black spot glowing gray under the white surface of rice.

"Well, check this out." She picked up the unlabeled jar. "The ignored jar has three mold spots. See? Which proves that negative attention is better than no attention at all." The proud scientist smiled.

Normally I would have said something cynical.

"And," she picked up the third jar, "the Love jar hasn't any mold yet. Neat, huh?"

I nodded. This was the sort of thing she'd normally share with Dad, assuming rightly that I could care less.

"That is cool," I said.

"Yeah it is." She looked at me to see if she could continue. I stood there staring at her. She picked up her book. "Dr. Emoto says there's ancient power in words because words come from natural vibrations in the environment."

I thought of the word rhabdomyosarcoma written on the scrap of paper in my hand. What sort of vibrations did that word came from? I knew what it meant now. Soft tissue sarcomas — meaning cancerous tumors — found in muscles used for motion, and affecting young children and teens.

"And all matter," she continued excitedly, "including us, is made up of rapid vibrations of particles. There's nothing actually solid about matter. It's just constant motion. Which means all things, including us, are in a continual state of change." She looked at me, eyes wide. "That's wild, huh?"

"Wild," I agreed, thinking of that bump in her calf. It wasn't a ganglian cyst you could Bible thump away. It was a cancerous tumor.

"Which is why the vibrations of words can affect things. Dr. Emoto says even our intentions create energy fields that affect matter."

I remembered saying that she'd better be really sick, and my stomach did some slow flip.

"I have to take a message out to Mom," I said.

Maggie didn't respond. She was too busy carefully writing with her left hand.

Nervous, I knocked on Mom's studio door. The door was the color of an eggplant. The former shed now had a bank of floor-to-ceiling windows, a skylight, plumbing, a dark room added on. Its shingle siding was painted. She called it her sanctuary.

"Come in," she said.

The place, as usual, had the smoky smell of inks and dyes. Today there was the tang of turpentine.

"How's it going?" I said.

"I'm great because I finally came up with the design for the last banner. I'm going Oriental, putting mahogany brown Japanese characters along the border which I'll box in so they could also pass for Celtic." She was talking more to herself than me.

"And look at the pillowcases Maggie's done. Beautiful, huh? Birthday gift for her friend Sasha." Two pillowcases were hanging on a clothesline in the corner in shades of plum and blue.

"Nice." I took a breath.

"She does it all herself now. From coming up with the design to applying the ink — everything. Even does her own wash-ups, which I'm very thankful for. Did you ever see the ties she did for her teachers?"

"No." Okay, just say it. "We got a call from Dr. Astley's office. Maggie has an appointment with another doctor tomorrow at 9:45."

"Oh? What kind of doctor?" Eyes on her drawing, she wasn't fully listening.

"Well... an oncologist." I'd looked that up, too. It meant cancer doctor.

Mom's head jerked up. She was off her stool and moving toward me, her body suddenly rigid.

"Who called? Are they still on the phone? Why didn't you come and get me?"

"I... I... some receptionist just gave me the information. Thought I was Dad, I think."

She was a pacing animal now, back and forth along her cutting table, breathing through an open mouth.

The spacious, light-filled room was feeling real small.

"Bring me the phone."

I left, bounding across the lawn to the house and crumpling the note in my fist. Maggie was drawing a picture of her moldy rice and didn't even look up as I grabbed the cordless.

When I got back, Mom's face was flushed.

"Where's Maggie?" she asked.

"In the kitchen."

"Okay." She caught my eye, hanging on, as if she was expecting me to give her some kind of reassurance.

"They don't know anything yet," I lied and moved toward the door. "It's probably nothing."

"Yeah," said Mom, starting to dial the number. She turned her back to me and I was free to go, back to my music and organizing tomorrow's party.

Once I got downstairs I felt weird, like I'd abandoned Mom or something, and immediately went back up to watch through the sliding glass doors.

Framed in the studio windows, she paced as she spoke on the phone. I watched her stop, run a hand through her hair. Then she picked up a pen and wrote something down. A big word maybe.

Behind me Maggie said to her Hate jar, "You're stupid and ugly. And I hate you."

* * *

Maggie not only met with the oncologist the next day but also had an MRI. She lay on a table and got shoved into a metal capsule, a Magnetic Resonance Imaging machine.

She got to put headphones on and pick out music. The music choices were either classical or old bands she'd never heard of. She didn't know what to choose so Mom chose for her — the Beach Boys. But it was so loud in the machine, she couldn't really hear it anyway.

I know all this because Mom insisted I be tested, too. So I was inside the same roaring, thumping white tunnel, squinting to try to hear the guitar lines from the Grateful Dead.

It was weird. You had to take off anything metal because it would get ripped off your body, whip around the machine and beat you up. And you couldn't have any metal pins inside your body like holding a broken bone together because those would get ripped right out of your skin.

I'd swallowed a dime when I was six but thought that would be stupid to mention. But I was worried for a minute it had somehow gotten stuck in my gut somewhere and would come flying out my butt.

The day after our MRIs, Mom met with the oncologist to discuss the test results. Though Dad wasn't due home from his conference for another couple of days, he arrived late that evening. He didn't say a word when he came in the door, just dropped his bag and briefcase, hung up his coat.

I was there with Mom. Maggie was upstairs in bed. Mom and Dad hugged, Dad squeezing his eyes shut as he laid his face against her hair.

"You okay?" he said in a small voice, and she answered him with a deep breath.

"Where is she?" he asked as they pulled apart.

"Sleeping," said Mom.

Before he went upstairs to look in on Maggie, he squeezed my shoulder.

"Hi, Dad."

"Gray." He couldn't hold my eye. But I was relieved to see him. He was a scientist. He knew about cells and muscles and shit. He'd have some answers.

* * *

The track lighting overhead made three equidistant circles on the rectangular kitchen table. Mom and Dad sat across from each other, a hole of light between them that I imagined was a portal into another dimension. Arms crossed, I stood in the kitchen doorway, neither in nor out.

In a slow, somber voice, careful not to leave anything out, Mom relayed the doctor's words. I learned that there are four stages to cancer. Stages one and two had to do with the size of the tumors, stage three was when cancer cells had spread to the lymph nodes, and stage four was when it had invaded the rest of the body. My MRI results had scored a big fat zero. Maggie got the highest score possible.

I was waiting for Dad to interrupt Mom, ask some smart question that challenged the doctors' findings. But he just sat there, elbows on the table, head in his hands, staring dry-eyed into the empty pool of light. His head looked impossibly heavy.

"The oncologist," said Mom, crumpling up her napkin and then spreading it out on the table only to do it again, "said there was no point trying to treat her at this late a stage." She shook her head, eyes staring. "Surely there's things we can try, I said to him." She crumpled the napkin and then ironed it flat again.

From the doorway, it felt like I was watching a movie. Some sucky drama. Just the kind of movie Maggie hated and I secretly kind of liked.

"He said the best we can do is keep her comfortable with pain medication and…" Her voice rose. "Her favorite activities."

It was an ugly moment. Dad's head seemed to gain a pound.

"He's going to give us some prescriptions to see what works best. What has the least side effects."

The movie set loomed bright. I could hear the violins moving into a minor key, my stomach along with them.

I'd never seen my parents look so helpless before. Made me feel real sketchy.

"I thought we might get her a kitten," Mom said to her napkin as she crushed it again.

"Julia – " Dad began, finally lifting his head, but Mom kept going.

"She's always wanted a kitten but what with my allergies… but, hey, I can take medication. Join the pill-popping club." She laughed, kind of, and ironed flat what had become an infinity of paper wrinkles. "But then if Maggie got attached to it…" Mom's voice started to quaver. "It might make things harder – "

"Julia," said Dad. "We'll get a second opinion for starters. Don't get morbid."

Mom looked at him and nodded repeatedly. "Yes, a second opinion. A third, even. And there's lots of alternative cures out there that doctors don't even know about. You hear of miracle cures all the – "

"We'll keep her comfortable for now," said Dad. "I'll talk to a couple of profs I know in cancer research."

He sounded in control. It was going to be okay.

"And we won't tell Maggie," said Mom, still nodding.

"She knows they're looking for cancer, Julia. We should tell her the diagnosis but don't have to tell her the prognosis."

"Yes, not the prognosis." She continued nodding.

"You look tired, Mom," I said, wanting her to stop nodding already. I stepped across the threshold into the movie. "You wanna lie down? Or want some tea or something?" I'd only ever made tea for my mom on Mother's Day.

She looked up, as if she was startled to see me.

"Thanks, Gray, but I couldn't lie down." She smiled as if I was being silly and went back to her napkin. "Do you really think we should tell her the diag – " This time, as she spread the napkin flat, it ripped down the middle. She grabbed it, shoved it against her closed mouth and abruptly stood up, whipping around to face the doors to the deck.

She leaned her hands on the glass as if she wanted to push it out of its frame, she spoke in a monotone. "I asked the doctor what could have caused it and he said this sort of thing can begin in utero." Her voice went real soft. "In utero?"

Dad closed his eyes and rubbed his forehead. I picked up the kettle. I was going to make tea whether anyone wanted it or not because I needed something to do right about now. I let the water run, found the sound soothing and hoped they did, too. Then I filled up the kettle.

"He said some children can have a genetic predisposition for cancer," continued Mom, "and be particularly sensitive to environmental carcinogens." Her hands on the window became fists.

"It's nobody's fault, Julia." Dad got out of his chair to go to her, bumping awkwardly against the corner of the table.

Mom made a half cough, half sigh sound, as if someone had punched the air from her stomach. She was going to cry and my stomach clenched as if that might stop her.

Dad turned her from the window and she practically dropped into his arms. The sinister hiss of the kettle filled the room. I willed the water to hurry up and boil so I could get this over with and go downstairs.

"It's okay," said Dad. "It's going to be okay." He didn't sound very convincing.

Mom started to sob, loud and clumsy sounding, while I stood there, holding a tea bag by its tiny string.

6   The C-Word

Back downstairs, I had to tell someone what was happening. Unload this shitty information. I called Davis and got the answering machine. He didn't have a cellphone. Davis's dad's new wife was events coordinator for her church and was always on the phone, even at nine-thirty at night.

I tried a few more times, then called Natalie instead.

"Hey, Nat."

"Hi, Gray. Guess what? I'm getting my hair highlighted."

"Oh, yeah?"

"Guess what color."

"God, I don't know. Blonde?"

"Blonde? Are you insane? With my skin? Guess again, though you'll never."

I wasn't really up for guessing games. "Green?"

"Green? No, you goof. Midnight blue."

"Wow. Sounds great."

"I thought of just getting it hennaed but saw this girl in a magazine with black hair like mine and dark blue highlights. It looked so great. A little out there, but not freakish or anything. My mom even likes the idea."

"It'll go great with your eyes," I said, trying to please her.

"You don't sound very enthusiastic."

"Oh, well, it's just that we've had some weird news."

"Really? What is it? You can tell me, Gray."

"It's my sister, Maggie. She's got this kind of cancer."

"Cancer? Are you kidding me? That's awful. I mean how bad is it? She's only like eleven."

"Twelve and it's stage four which is pretty bad. She had an MRI scan thing. I had to get one, too."

"Do you have it?"

"No, it was just a precaution."

"You better not have it," she said, as if she'd be pissed if I did.

"Yeah."

"So, like, does she have a tumor?" Natalie asked in a small voice.

"A lot more than one, I think. They're in her muscles."

"Ew, God."

This was followed by silence. I didn't know what I expected her to do or say. Something, anything, to make it feel less real.

"I'm sorry, Gray," she said, "but I got to get off. My mom's calling me."

"Yeah, sure, go on."

"I hope your sister gets better and I'm so glad that you're all right."

"Thanks."

"See you at school."

"Yeah. Did you think of where you want to go for dinner?" I asked, wanting to end on a more positive note.

"No, I'm still thinking."

"Okay. See you."

"Bye."

"Bye."

I thought it would make me feel better telling someone. It didn't.

*　*　*

Like usual, Davis stopped by on his way to school so we could walk together. It was overcast and cold, the sky the color of a dirty sheet. The wind stung my face. The day felt mean, and enjoying it.

"How ya doing?" I said. I was feeling pretty messed. Mom was inside making an appointment with another oncologist. A second opinion. Her eyes were puffy and red, like she'd been up all night crying.

"I'm cool." His feet pranced around as he boxed one, two at the air. "Where's Maggie?" he asked, since she usually left for school the same time as me. The middle school was just across the field from the high school. Mom insisted we walk together, more or less. He turned around to pretend-punch me.

"She's got a doctor's appointment."

Then I told him. Made the mistake of using the word "terminal."

Davis stopped, his jaw muscles bulging as he ground his teeth together. He kicked at the grass beside the sidewalk and a clump of turf went flying.

"Holy shit. Why's life so messed up?"

"It might not be that bad," I said, only because I felt rotten now to have dumped this on him. "It was just one guy's opinion."

"Yeah, well, she's young. That should help."

When I'd looked up Maggie's type of cancer, I'd found out that being young actually made things worse. In old people tumors grew slowly precisely because old people didn't do anything fast. In the young and otherwise healthy, tumors took off running. I didn't tell him this, and we walked a little ways in silence.

"Mom's going to research alternative cures. Says there's a lot of stuff out there doctors don't know about."

"Good. That's good. Anything I can do?" He sounded desperate.

I shrugged. We didn't say anything more. But that was all right. I actually felt a bit better. I suddenly remembered one of those dumb Chuck Norris jokes and wondered if he was thinking of it, too.

Chuck Norris's tears cure cancer. Too bad he's never cried.

* * *

On my way to second block, I passed Natalie at her locker. Erin and Chrissy were with her.

"Hey, Nat," I said.

"Hi, Gray."

Her friends turned, looked at me, then looked down or away. They seemed to form a wall around her.

"Want to grab a slice today with Davis and me?"

She was wearing a blue V-neck sweater, the purple

lace of the bra I'd come to know and love beckoning at the V.

"Yeah, okay."

"Meet you at the bleachers then?"

"Okay." The shield of girl still hadn't moved, otherwise I would have slipped a kiss to her neck. I could tell by their shifty glances that they had a secret. My secret? I guess it was okay if Natalie told them. Word would get around soon enough. Still, it seemed too quick, and I was glad Maggie didn't go to this school.

Erin, Davis, Natalie and I had pizza together. Nat, as usual, kept the conversation going. She talked about her hair appointment and what happened on the *Lost* episode which my family had forgotten to watch.

Davis looked pained by the sound of her voice and said nothing, while I did my best to nod and smile despite the fact that she was directing her words more at Erin than me. We didn't mention Maggie. I think she was trying to take my mind off it, make things seem normal.

The next day I ran into Ciel. She was with a fedora-wearing girl named Ginny who played trumpet in the school jazz band.

"Hey," I said when she glanced up.

"Gray. God, I heard about your sister." Word *had* spread fast. "I'm really sorry." Her face looked genuinely pained.

"Yeah, thanks."

She reached out and stroked my arm, real soft. It felt surreally good to be touched so soft like that.

When I got home, Mom, who was never not busy

doing something, was just sitting at the kitchen table staring out the window.

"Hey, Mom. You okay?" I dropped my backpack into a chair.

"Second opinion wasn't any better," she said, still staring. "And Dad's friends at work. Just as dire."

"That sucks."

"Talk to her, Gray." Mom turned to me, her tone pleading. "See how she's doing. But *don't* use the C-word!"

"The C-word?"

"Here, you can take her up a glass of water and a couple of these turmeric pills."

"Isn't that what goes in curry?" I remembered Parmjot's mom once making chicken with turmeric and dates. It was delicious, even though I got the runs after.

"Yes, it's an East Indian spice. There's something in it that shrinks tumors." She forced a smile.

"Really? Are the words tumor and turmer – "

"It's just something I'm trying. I talked to a friend of a friend whose husband had a stomach tumor the size of a grapefruit and he…" Her voice trailed off. "Well, it's gone now. There's lots of things to try." She pointed an accusing finger at me. "Lots of things and I'm starting with this."

"Sounds great. I'll take it to her," I said and got the hell out of there.

I don't think I'd stepped in Maggie's room for like two years. Against a backdrop of swamp-green walls, it was decorated with all the silkscreen things she'd made with

Mom over the years: curtains, matching canopy over her bed, pillows, a decorative kite up in one corner, a shawl over the back of her desk chair, picture frames...

"Hey, Maggot," I said, but said it nice.

"Hi."

She was bent over the floor cutting out stuff, chick music playing on her iDog while grotesque close-ups of insects flashed on her screen saver.

Maggie loved bugs, the bug zoo her favorite outing as a little kid. Dad used to take us both. Maggie would hold the tarantula, let the stick bug creep up her arm, the praying mantis, while I stayed tucked behind Dad, my skin crawling.

"Brought you some water."

"Thanks. The pills I'm taking make me really thirsty." She reached for the water.

"Oh, and Mom wanted me to give you these." I held out the capsules filled with mustard-colored powder.

She took one look at them and just took the water. "They're too big to swallow."

She chugged it, plunked the glass on the floor and went back to cutting out what looked like the letter N. I started to put the pills on her desk.

"Don't step on my poster!"

"I won't. Jeez, you scared me."

"I'm cutting out the title for my project. Dad thinks I should call it Mind Matters but I like Matter Minds better. Makes you stop and think."

"Sure, that's good." I couldn't begin to stop and think. "So, uh, how *are* you feeling?" I put the pills down.

"Okay, I guess, considering I've got cancer everywhere." She shrugged.

"Oh."

"I like finally knowing what it is. I had a feeling it might be something weird." She finished cutting the N, laid it next to the I and scrunched up her nose. "Cancer is defined as an uncontrolled growth of cells that differ structurally and biochemically from the normal cells of the tissue of origin."

And Mom thought we'd keep her in the dark?

She picked up the N again and began to trim it.

"I wonder why that happens?" She sounded genuinely curious.

"Yeah." A fat brown spider, its back covered in a thousand baby versions of itself, flashed on the screen saver. I shivered.

"It makes sense that there's a catalyst of some kind. For every action a reaction and all that."

"I guess so."

"Will you get me more water?" Maggie held up her glass.

"Yeah, sure."

"Cancer's not all bad," she said.

"What?"

"You're bringing me water." She snickered and turned back to her cutting. "Like you're my slave now."

"And you're still a nerdy brat." I smiled, too, then noticed my camera on her dresser. She'd borrowed it to take progressive pictures of her rotting rice.

I picked it up, turned it on.

"Hey, Maggot." She lifted her face and smiled big and ugly, showing her teeth. The tooth to the right of her big tooth was chipped from when I tripped her and she fell and knocked it on the coffee table, about four years back. I thought it was funny back then.

I took her picture. Wondered how many more of her there'd be to take.

Downstairs I told Mom that Maggie seemed amazingly chill about the whole thing.

She shook her head.

"Well, she can't really know what it means. Not at her age. I'll go see if she wants a snack."

"Uh, she didn't take those pills. Said they were too big."

"Okay. Maybe I'll mix it in with juice."

That taste would be impossible to hide, I thought, but didn't say anything. I got myself a bowl of cereal and went downstairs. I wanted to load some tunes onto my iPod but Maggie's words, *for every action a reaction*, kept skipping through my head.

That first doctor said something about environmental causes, didn't he? I mean, what if Mom's turmeric stuff did get rid of the tumors but the shit that caused them in the first place was still around? Then Maggie would just keep growing new ones, wouldn't she?

That was logical, I thought, proud for thinking like a scientist for once. If you've got lung cancer, you stop smoking as well as getting radiation and stuff. And not to be selfish about it, but whatever Maggie was exposed to, I was, too. And Mom and Dad.

I went into Google and typed in the words: Rhabdomyosarcoma, Causes.

7 Rhaby

There were a frickin' million sites to navigate. I decided to stick to legitimate-sounding ones – American Cancer Society, Cancer Prevention Coalition, Mount Sinai Pediatric Hospital – skimmed the scientific treatise shit, then cut and pasted stuff that made sense to me into a file named Rhaby. I imagined I was a detective digging for clues, and that if I dug deep enough I just might find the answer, meaning the cause.

I mean, why Maggie and not me or one of her friends?

I came across a list of "known and suspect" carcinogens by the American Cancer Society. It was a mile long.

70,000 synthetic chemicals are in production today. Many are suspected to cause cancer or other health effects, but only 600 have been adequately tested. Even fewer have been tested for how they react with other chemicals.

What the hell were all these chemicals for? 70,000? There were only 365 days in a year.

Rhabdomyosarcoma affects four out of every million children. The disease has been linked to exposure to dioxins, PAHs (polycyclic aromatic hydrocarbons), vinyl chloride, benzene, asbestos, and others.

Okay, so maybe one of these chemicals had found its way into our house in some serious way? I'd do a process of elimination. I'd start with Dioxins and then work my way to Other.

Dioxins are extremely poisonous and known to cause nervous disorders, skin diseases, cancer and birth defects.

Burning garbage created dioxins, I found out, specifically the burning of plastics. Then why was garbage thrown out in plastic bags?

Dioxins from incinerated garbage are carried for hundreds of miles on tiny specks of fly ash landing on farmland and ingested by livestock.

It said that dioxins were fat soluble, so the main contact with them was eating beef and dairy products. Maggie was a serious carnivore. Loved burgers and steak, put melted cheese on everything. I was more of a chicken man. So maybe it was her diet.

Note: Cut out beef and dairy.

Chicken and pork have the third and fourth highest levels of dioxin contamination just below beef and dairy products.

Oh… Note: Eat fish.

Dioxin levels in fish are 100,000 times that of the surrounding environment.

Okay, forget it. Become vegetarian.

Chlorine based pesticides and herbicides sprayed on fruits and vegetables can contain dioxins.

God, was nothing safe to eat?

Note: Wash and peel stuff.

The bleaching of paper products at pulp and paper mills produces dioxins and products contaminated with dioxins.

The stack of paper in my printer suddenly looked evil. We had tons of bleached paper products in the house. Toilet paper, Kleenex, napkins, paper towels, books, magazines. But we didn't eat those things. Dad and Mom used white coffee filters in the coffee machine but Maggie didn't drink coffee. Kleenex went up your nose and toilet paper went, well... whatever, it couldn't be good for you.

Note: Buy unbleached paper products.

I moved on to PAHs.

In Canada alone, fourteen million kilograms of carcinogens are released into the air every year from car exhaust and the burning of municipal waste.

What the... I thought cars were just a CO_2 problem. I looked it up.

Car exhaust contains three types of carcinogens: PAHs, benzene and formaldehyde.

Why the hell didn't anybody talk about that? Wasn't last year's Run for the Cure at our school sponsored by some car company?

Note: Maggie's room was at the front of the house above the garage. Don't start car in garage. Park on the street.

Burning wood creates dangerous PAHs.

Dad often made a fire in the evening – just last night, in fact – and Maggie loved to read sprawled in front it.

Note: Don't use fireplace.

I thought I'd probably covered it, but just in case went onto the next suspect chemical: vinyl chloride.

Plastic PVC pipes manufactured before 1977 can leach vinyl chloride into your water.

Our pipes, which I'd seen in the storage room and under the kitchen sink, were made of black plastic. I'd ask Dad about it.

The breakdown of chlorinated chemicals in drinking water can form vinyl chloride.

So then the pipes didn't even matter.

"Dinner time," Mom called from the top of the stairs.

I lifted my head from the screen. Man… this was more complicated than I thought.

* * *

Mom had made one of Maggie's favorite dinners: spareribs, mashed potatoes and peas, ice cream sundaes for dessert. To keep up Maggie's spirits, I guess. She'd even lit candles and used cloth napkins like she did for special occasions, only it was just another Wednesday night.

I couldn't help wondering what the serving of dioxins was in this meal. Spareribs were like fifty percent fat, there was milk in the potatoes, and the potatoes themselves were no doubt grown with pesticides as were the peas.

I suddenly wasn't hungry.

I watched Maggie chew a rib clean to the bone.

"Sasha's birthday's next weekend," she told Mom, picking up another. "A skating party, back to her place for dinner – hot chocolate and hot dogs – then a sleepover."

"Are you sure you're up for it?" asked Mom.

"I'm not missing it."

"I didn't mean – "

"I'm not as sore since I started taking the pills."

She sank her teeth into a second fat-filled rib. I tried not watch.

"We're going to do the Ouiji board. Have a séance," she said through a mouthful of pig fat.

"Hot dogs cause cancer," I blurted, unable to say what I was really thinking because it would ruin Mom's fancy dinner. I couldn't remember what it was in hot dogs, but my grade five teacher used to check our lunches for ham or baloney, which also had it. She made us all afraid of our sandwiches.

"They contain nitrites and nitrates," said Maggie, one step ahead of me as usual.

"I think it's all right once in a while," said Dad, smiling at her.

"I'll just have one," she said reasonably.

I didn't say anything, just ate my potatoes and peas. I couldn't eat the ribs. Dad and Maggie chatted about Mars and Venus being visible in the sky starting in a couple of weeks.

I thought of Natalie's sweet sixteen and how I'd be losing my V-card under Mars and Venus. That sounded all right.

"Are you going to eat those?" Maggie was pointing to my plate.

"Uh, no."

"Can I?"

"Sure." I passed her my plate, then felt all messed and guilty watching her scrape it onto hers.

Maggie didn't have room for the sundae and left the table to do homework. As soon as she was gone, Dad's cheeriness vanished and Mom sighed and ran her hand through her hair.

"I bought smaller capsules today to reduce the size of the turmeric pills. And I got a book out of the library that claims flax oil and cottage cheese works wonders for every kind and at every stage of – "

"You know," I interrupted, "a lot of cancers are caused by chemicals in the environment. I've been reading stuff on the net on Maggie's type. It kind of makes sense that she can't get better if she's still being exposed to what made her sick in the first place."

Mom and Dad just stared at me. It was probably the most words in a row they'd heard out of me all year.

"Bodies heal if given the chance," I added, quoting some catchy phrase I'd come across.

Dad, the scientist, smiled what I took to be a patronizing smile. "It's a moot point, Gray, worrying about the cause at this junc – "

"No, go on, Gray," said Mom, holding up a hand to shush Dad. "I want to hear what you've found out."

"Well, dioxins, for example. We get them in our blood from eating meat. But also chicken and pork. Fish, too. So I thought we might consider going vegetarian." I was waiting for Dad to interrupt me, correct me, but he didn't.

"We could do that," said Mom. "No harm in that."

"We could also start buying unbleached paper products which can be contaminated with dioxins."

"That's a question of parts per million," said Dad. "Hardly worth worrying about."

"Still, parts can add up," said Mom, staring at me. "What else, Gray?"

"Well, chlorinated water can create vinyl chloride which is another chemical indicated in Maggie's cancer. So we might get some sort of filter system."

"Gray, sweetheart, this is really thoughtful of you," she cooed and sat up straighter in her chair. "I like these ideas. It'll be healthier for Maggie and for us, too."

"Also if our pipes were manufactured before 1977 – "

"It's a little too late to think – " started Dad.

"It's not too late," Mom snapped, startling me. "I cannot sit here, Ethan," – she banged her hands on the table – "and believe there's nothing to do but watch my child get sicker."

"She's *your* child now?" he said.

Whoa. This was the closest thing I'd seen to my parents having an argument. They'd gone all stiff and alert.

"We can just try and eliminate some stuff," I said, breaking the silence. "Maybe there's like one thing – "

"It's never one thing, Gray." Dad sounded exasperated now.

"I mean, that put her body over the edge. Messed with her immune system."

Mom turned to face me, her back to Dad. "I'll look into water systems tomorrow, Gray. And I'll go back to the library and get some vegetarian cookbooks." It was the most hopeful I'd seen her since we got the news, which made me feel good.

"Buying organic stuff would be good since pesticides can contain dioxins," I added.

"Absolutely," said Mom.

"And, well, I didn't realize that car exhaust contains so many carcinogens."

"It would be nice to get all the cars off the road but a little difficult," said Dad, no longer smiling.

"I was just thinking how Maggie's room is right above the gar – "

"So we'll park on the street from now on," said Mom.

She got up and came around to my side of the table, put her hands on my shoulders and kissed the top of my head.

"This is great, Gray. I'll work on finding a cure and you work on finding the cause. Teamwork," she said, emphasizing the word.

I felt like some kind of hero. Dad gave me a sad smile.

"I don't mean to discourage you, Gray. Or you, Julia," he said gently. "I just don't want people getting their hopes – "

"Maybe she shouldn't go to that party," said Mom.

"Let her go to the party," said Dad, voice rising. "How many more parties will she – "

"Don't say it, Ethan. Just don't say it." Her hands tightened on my shoulders, her nails digging in painfully.

*   *   *

Davis, Hughie and I walked over to Maggie's middle school to get her homework. She'd stayed home, a bad headache on top of her other aches. Mom thought it might be a side effect of the pain pills.

I thought it might be detox. We hadn't eaten meat for four days.

"You know that new car smell?" I asked.

"I love that smell," said Davis. "My mother's first husband's kid just bought a new Camaro. White with black interior. It's seriously dice and reeks of that – "

"I heard," said Hughie, "that dealers actually spray that smell in cars. To keep them smelling new."

"I want to get some," said Davis, excited. "Spray my bedroom, the inside of my pants – "

"That smell is off-gas and it's carcinogenic. Spraying fragrance on top of it's even worse 'cause they're made of hundreds of chemicals, none of them tested together or – "

"You're getting really into this," said Hughie.

"Yeah, and it's pretty messed up, too. Did you know that some carpeting's treated with pesticides?"

"My grandmother uses this killer stuff on her lawn every spring," laughed Hughie. "She has to post this little warning sign on her lawn for animals and kids to stay off it or die."

"Pesticides are linked to tons of cancers," I said.

"She believes dandelions are Satan's tears." He laughed again, though I didn't get what was so funny.

"I mean, carcinogens are like everywhere. Drywall, particle board and plywood are all preserved with formaldehyde which is right there on the American Cancer

Society's list." I stabbed the air. "And it off-gasses for years, so we're all breathing it in."

"Why's it in there?" asked Davis.

"It keeps stuff from going moldy, which my dad says would be just as toxic. But still there's got to be something else."

"Hey, you know that job I applied for at the grocery store?" said Hughie. "I have an interview on Saturday. Which my brother says means I've probably got the job."

"Make sure you don't smell in the interview," said Davis. "And wash your greasy hair for a change, you animal. And keep your ass in your pants."

Hughie laughed. "Have you seen that short on YouTube with the guy mooning – "

"New stats say everyone, meaning a hundred percent of people who live past the age of seventy, will get cancer."

"There goes Grandma," said Hughie.

"It's not funny," I said.

"You're not funny," he said. "I'm outa here. See you tomorrow."

"Asshole," I said when Hughie was out of earshot.

"People don't like to think about that stuff," said Davis.

"Well, that's the problem, isn't it?" I veered off onto the path to Maggie's school.

"Play on line later," called Davis.

"Yeah, maybe."

Stepping inside the school, I looked at the vinyl linoleum, the particle board ceiling, the drywall halls and held my breath.

I collected Maggie's math book plus some homework sheets and wondered if dioxin from the paper could get absorbed through my hands. Felt like I should be wearing gloves, a face mask of some kind. I was major claustrophobic suddenly and needed air.

As I shoved open the nearest exit, the short bus was idling ten feet away, plumes of toxic exhaust stinking up the air.

Get me out of here.

8   Hope and Fear

I cornered Natalie outside the gym after the rest of the class had gone in. Kissed her long and hard, a hand slipping over one beautiful breast, my head going all light. Balloon head.

"Want to hang tomorrow after school? Come over to my place?" Tomorrow was Friday, but I no longer felt like having the gang over. In fact, I was thinking maybe Nat and I didn't have to wait until her parents went away. Yesterday I'd stolen a couple of condoms from Dad's sock drawer.

I nosed under her hair and kissed her neck. Her shampoo smelled just like mangoes. I thought of how many hundreds of sketchy chemicals combined to make that smell…

No. Don't think about it.

"Oh," she sighed, "my mom won't let me come over."

I lifted my head. "What do you mean?"

"Well, Maggie and all."

"She's not contagious, you know."

"My mom's just really cautious about stuff like that." She shrugged.

"She thinks our house is toxic or something?" It was what I was starting to think.

"I don't know. She's just weird."

"Then how about your place?"

"Actually, I'm going shopping with Erin. I want to buy a couple of shirts that'll match my hair. I'm getting it done tomorrow, remember? Maybe we can do something tomorrow night?"

"I work Saturday."

"Oh, yeah. And I work Sunday." She slipped out from under my arm. "Come on, we better go. We'll be late for class."

"Are we still on for dinner and…?" I didn't know how to say it without sounding like some crude animal.

She turned to me. "I can go out with you, just not home with you." She kissed me then, did her tongue routine, and I felt a little better.

* * *

Saturday I woke up to the singe-your-nose-hair smell of Dasha's aerosols. It hit me. Maybe it was something *she* used that triggered the cancer. Who knew what was in those cleaners?

I got out of bed, threw some clothes on. In the rec room, I excused myself and asked Dasha, real nice like, if I could see her spray bottles.

She looked at me with her beautiful sad eyes. "My bottle?"

Sergei stopped sweeping the ceiling corners.

"You going to clean for us?" he asked, drilling those

consonants. He held out his broom, angling the handle toward my face.

"No, no. I'm, uh, just doing a study of what's in those sprays," I said, thinking, please don't push that into my brain.

He lowered his broom and, still looking at me, gestured to Dasha to hand them over.

"Thanks, great."

None of the bottles' ingredients were listed. Not one. I took note of the brands – to look up on line – and quickly gave Dasha back her aerosols. I held up my hands to show Sergei I didn't mean anything by it.

* * *

Dressed in my Cineplex worker bee uniform – black pants, blinding yellow shirt and black ball cap with yellow logo – I planned to hit the mall early to shop for a birthday present for Natalie. I'd blown it on the Christmas present thing. She gave me this dice shirt and a leather wallet and I gave her a gift certificate to the Cineplex. Dickhead.

I went to ask Mom for ideas but found her bent over the kitchen counter, phone tucked between her ear and shoulder, concentrating on filling little clear capsules with turmeric powder while making excuses, by the sound of it, for being behind on those banners for the bank. I didn't have time to wait so went upstairs to ask Maggie. She was a girl, after all.

Propped up in bed typing on her laptop, Maggie had purplish rings under her eyes. Hot dog rings, I thought. She'd gone to that sleepover. Probably had pop at the theater. I'd found out that pop often contained benzene, which was used in cleaning the cans and dispensers.

"What is that?" On her bed table beside a glass of reverse osmosis water (Mom had had a system installed) and her water crystal book was a bowl of cottage cheese sitting in a pool of yellow oil.

"Some cancer cure of Mom's. It's disgusting."

It did look disgusting, but…

"We got to get you well, so just eat it, okay?"

"I'll probably just throw it up anyway."

"You'll get used to the taste."

"Yeah," she said, sounding noncommittal.

"Mag, do you have any idea what I could buy Natalie for a present?"

She stopped what she was doing.

"Bracelets. Those thin metal ones that come in different colors. Girls wear them in bunches. Like twenty on one arm. They make this neat tinkling sound."

"Hey, good idea," I said.

She typed something. "Go for the silver ones, not the gold. Silver's in right now. Oh, and matching hoop earrings."

"Okay. Sounds good."

"The earrings shouldn't be too big. About like this." She made a circle with her thumb and middle finger.

I nodded, was about to leave when she said, "I really want to see the next Harry Potter movie."

For a minute I wondered if she was saying she wanted to live to see it. She'd read all the books at least twice. I'd only seen the movies, and afterward Maggie would fill me in, explaining things the movie left out.

"I could take you to the preview," I offered. I'd always taken Davis, Parm or Hughie before. Maggie looked at me sideways. It was a pity move and she knew it.

"Okay, as long as none of my friends find out." She smiled and I laughed.

"Maggot head," I said, leaving.

"Was it your dumb idea to go vegetarian?" she called after me.

* * *

I found the bracelets Maggie was talking about, in silver, and got several dark blue ones, too, to match Natalie's hair. She'd just had it done and had sent me a message saying how great it looked. There were a million different sizes of hoop earrings, so I was glad Maggie had been specific.

When I told the saleslady it was a gift, she hunted up a little white box with that cotton stuff, laid the earrings inside the bracelets. It looked really nice. She even put a ribbon around it so I didn't have to worry about how to wrap it.

At work, behind the refreshment counter, I filled up paper cup after paper cup of Coke, Orange Crush or Sprite. Benzene drinks, was how I started to think of them. Cancer colas. And when I wasn't doing that I was drizzling cancerous hydrogenated fat over popcorn. Or selling neon candy full of cancerous food coloring.

Handing a combo tray of pop, popcorn and candy bag to one little wide-eyed kid after another, I felt like some serial killer.

At the end of the night, I was the one told to haul seven black plastic bags out to the dumpster. Seven. Would they be incinerated and spray dioxin confetti everywhere?

As I was leaving, the manager was giving out boxes of Reeses Cups because their due date was coming up.

"Any takers?" he asked. "They'll get thrown out otherwise."

Everyone took a box. There was one left.

"Gray?" he asked.

Maggie loved Reeses Cups. I imagined her face lighting up.

"Yeah, sure. Thanks."

Maggie was already asleep when I got home. So I looked up chocolate and cancer on the net. It checked out all right.

Then I looked up peanuts and cancer. Shit. Peanuts had a naturally occurring carcinogen called aflatoxin. And because peanuts needed so little soil depth, some crops were being grown on landfill sites. No wonder there were so many damn peanut allergies.

I dumped the Reeses Cups in the garbage, pumped up some music and went on MSN to see if Nat was on. She wasn't, but I wrote and told her I'd bought her a birthday present.

it'll match your hair, which I can't wait 2 c... and kiss. can already picture how great it looks.

I signed off, then remembered reading something about hair dye and cancer. Too late now.

9 Happy Valley

The next morning, Maggie was feeling good so Dad and Mom were taking her and a friend to the science center. Afterwards they were going to have lunch at this famous vegetarian restaurant. They asked if I wanted to go, too. Yeah, right. I was glad Mom and Dad were going together, though, because they weren't talking a lot lately.

Normally on a Sunday I would hang with friends, do some gaming, hike up in the woods and smoke some leaf. Davis and Parmjot had both called to see what I was doing. It was even sunny out. A decent March day. But I wanted to finish what I'd started. Clean house, so to speak.

I cranked up my iPod and went room to room with my list of suspect chemicals and a bucket to put stuff in.

Every shampoo, soap and detergent in the house contained DEA or TEA – a chemical that made things foamy and slippery – both of which led to the formation of the nasty NDEA. Cancer. Dad's cover-the-gray shampoo had coal tars. Cancer. Mom's disinfectant spray contained orthophenylphenol. Cancer. The bathroom cleanser contained crystalline silica. Cancer. The whitening tooth-paste Natalie insisted I start using had about three things on the list. Maggie had started using it, too. I put it in the bucket.

I gave up trying to match up all the ingredients and just started including anything with long unpronounceable names. I included all the bleached-paper stuff and any food with hydrogenated fat in it, nitrates and nitrites, BHA and BHT, and food colorings. I emptied my bucket onto the kitchen table. When that was full, I used the counters.

By the time Dad, Mom and Maggie and friend came home, I was pretty tired.

Maggie and her friend, Tess, came in the kitchen and grabbed some water.

"Hey, Gray," said Maggie. "Mind if we watch this in your suite? She held up a movie. I knew she knew she was making the most of being sick but still I said, "Sure."

"Kitchen's a mess," she said, glancing at the counters before disappearing downstairs.

"What do we have here?" said Dad.

"I've collected all the stuff with sketchy chemicals in them," I said, pretty proud of myself. Having sacrificed my day and all.

"Oh, yeah?"

"It's amazing how much garbage is in stuff. I thought if we cleared it all out and – "

"Gray, it's trace amounts of these chemicals." Dad picked up my deodorant. "Deemed safe in amounts tested by scientists."

"Trace amounts don't make them less carcinogenic."

"And some molecules, like titanium dioxide, for example," he said, reading a tube of sunscreen, "are too big to penetrate blood vessels."

"But skin cancer happens on the surface."

"What I mean to say, Gray, is that you just don't know enough to be making these decisions."

"I've been reading on the net — "

"Don't believe everything you read." He sighed. "Especially on line."

He was treating me like I was some little kid.

Mom was now standing in the doorway all glassy-eyed. She looked seriously sleep-deprived.

"I know you're just trying to help, Gray," said Dad. "But a bigger help would be to remember to take out the trash so I didn't have to do it for you." He snickered. "Or we'll put you in charge of the recycling?" He started to put the cereal back in the cupboard and I felt my stomach harden. I'd blown off my day to do this…

"You have to be practical, Gray, weigh the negatives against the benefits," he continued. "The sun can cause cancer but we still need it to survive. Tuna fish has mercury in it but that doesn't mean it isn't one of the most nutritious things you can eat. Heck, there's DDT, dioxins and whatever else being found in breast milk, but nobody would argue it still isn't hands down the best thing for a baby."

"Breast milk has carcinogens?" The thought made me queasy. "And nobody's doing anything about it?"

"You are, Gray," said Mom, walking past Dad to grab some plastic bags. "And it's just great. I'm going to go, right now, and return these things for healthier alternatives."

Dad glared at her back. "Well, you're not taking my shampoo."

"Coal tars are on the American Cancer Society list," I said, more confident with Mom on side.

Shampoo in hand, Dad met my eye. "The plastic of your iPod there is made using hundreds of chemical compounds. The cotton in your goddamn brand-name clothes is the most heavily pesticided crop in the world."

I don't think I'd ever heard Dad swear in front of me before.

"The creature comforts of this modern world come with a price, Gray."

"Cancer?"

He threw up his hands.

"You want to live like a caveman, go right ahead. It'll save me some money." He smiled but it wasn't funny.

"Ethan," said Mom, sounding disappointed. "We're all working toward the same objective – "

"We all need to relax is what we need to do." He sounded anything but relaxed.

"Relax?" said Mom in disbelief. "Relax?"

"Yes, and enjoy Maggie while we still – "

"This is no time to relax."

Dad shook his head. "I give up."

"Great attitude." She started jamming things in a shopping bag.

Dad took his tainted shampoo and left.

"Sorry, Mom." Though I was pissed at Dad, I hated to see them argue.

"No, you are not sorry," she said sternly. "It only makes sense to err on the safe side. Right?"

"Well, yeah."

"Come on, help me bag. I'm going to return these things."

"Can you return stuff that's already been used?"

"I don't see why not." She sounded ready for a fight.

*   *   *

I'm not sure how, but Mom managed to return every last item and arrived home with organic this and that, non-toxic cleansers, unbleached toilet paper, etc.

"Had quite the public argument with the manager," she said, laughing. She seemed all hopped. "People were stopping to watch but what did I care?"

Sure glad I wasn't there.

"I want to drive out to this organic farm my friend Kath told me about. Their food's supposed to have life-giving properties." She was talking really fast. "Why don't you come with me, Gray? You can practice your highway driving."

"Shouldn't we put these groceries away?"

"We can do that after. Let's go before it gets too late. Their stand closes at four, I think."

"Yeah, sure." I wasn't doing anything and I'd only ever driven on the highway once before. It was sick to go that fast.

After pulling out of the driveway, I gave the car that burst of gas for that rush of accelerating from a stop.

A few minutes down the road, it dawned on me that whenever I hit the gas, I was pumping out a hit of carcinogens. I pulled up to a stoplight thinking how the guy on his bike beside us was inhaling my exhaust, and the kid on the corner being pushed in her stroller. Her little nose was happily sucking it all in.

Man, I hated knowing this shit.

I tried to ease off on the gas after that, take advantage of hills and coast as much as possible.

"I read about this substance," said Mom. "Oh, what's its name? Something fruits and vegetables produce to fight off pests and molds. It's found just under the skin and has cancer-fighting properties. Is even marketed as a cure." She waved her hand, knocking the rearview mirror. She didn't notice so I fixed it. "Sprayed produce doesn't have to work to fight off pests so it doesn't produce the substance. Or much of it. Oh, what's it called…"

Up ahead I could see the light turn yellow. Normally I'd race up to an intersection and more or less ram on the brakes, but I took my foot off the gas and let the car coast the rest of the way to what was now a red light.

"I'm going to start cooking more," Mom went on. "Not just dinner, but breakfast, too. Even your lunches. No more fast food."

We were going slug slow. If I timed it right, I might just get to the light as it turned green again and never actually come to a stop. The guy behind me laid on the horn and Mom jumped.

"What was that?"

"Some jerk wanting to hurry up and stop."

* * *

Over the weathered roadside stand read a hand-carved sign: *Produce That Makes You Happy.* Were these people so old school they didn't even know enough to call their stuff organic?

It was real quiet. Maybe spring came earlier to the country, because there were pale green buds on bushes and trees, something I hadn't noticed happening in town, and white snowdrops bloomed along the base of the produce stand.

Built on a slope, the farm backed onto a wooded park where we used to go for family hikes when Maggie and I were little. There was a creek running down the west side that we used to dam with rocks. We'd make pretend boats out of sticks and race them to the dam. From the top of the park you could see all the way downtown.

"Lovely afternoon," said the woman working the stand.

"Yes," said Mom. "Yes, it is. Heard terrific things about your produce."

The woman just smiled. A thick mash of gray curls raged on her head like a small storm. She had these weird eyes, one brown and one pale blue, like a husky's. Her gaze was steady as a dog's, too. In contrast to the tense, jerky movements of my mother as she tested vegetables, this woman didn't move a muscle. For a minute I imagined this was on purpose, to try and calm my mom down. It was strange watching them together.

Being only March, there wasn't that much to choose from: green leafy things I didn't know the names of, chives, some squashes, onions, eggs, jars of jam, tomato sauce and various pickled things. There was a basket of muffins for a dollar each. At the end of the table were these doll-sized pillows. Above the pillows was a small sign that read *Happy Valley Farm: Nacie and Milan Daskaloff.* A small *Help Wanted* sign hung above that.

"And you're Nacie?" said Mom, pointing at the sign.

"I am."

"And you grow all this yourself?"

"With my husband, Milan."

"Must be an awful lot of work. I've always wanted to grow vegetables but it's hard to find the time." Mom rattled away, holding a bouquet of chives to her nose. She had a stiff plastic smile on her face but I didn't think she realized it.

"I'm Julia, by the way, and this is my son, Gray."

"Julia," she repeated with a nod. "And Gray." She was studying me with her calm two-tone eyes when this chicken shot out of nowhere, leapt on my foot and banged its beak into my knee.

"Ow!" I yelled, shaking it off.

"Cla-rence," said Nacie slowly, and the bird tucked in its red neck, guilty as hell, and ran off, ass feathers trembling. "Means he trusts you," she said as I rubbed the front of my knee. Clarence, I guess, was a rooster, not a chicken. "He'd peck you in the back of the knee if he didn't."

Flattering. Knee throbbing, I checked my jeans for blood. Nacie just smiled at me.

Up the lane, I could see their farmhouse with its sweeping front porch and a laundry line of swaying sheets that ran from the porch's corner to a tree. Nice, I thought, not using a dryer. There was an orchard to the right of the house and a pond with a giant weeping willow whose branch tips swept the water's surface. Farther up the slope were the growing fields and a couple of outbuildings painted bright red, which looked cool against the green.

I wished I'd brought my camera. I'd take a picture of this woman's wacky eyes for starters. And a close-up of that rooster's butt. The pond would be dope with all the reflections and shit. I had a sudden urge to bolt up the hill and climb that big-ass tree.

Coming down the lane toward the house was a gray-haired guy and what looked like a small horse. The man was dressed in a tweed cap, khaki pants tucked into high rubber boots, white button-down shirt and stretched-out brown cardigan. He looked like someone out of one of those English TV dramas.

The horse looked our way and barked a deep booming bark that echoed up the hillside. A dog? The man hushed him and turned in behind the laundry, the freak-dog following.

Mom bought some of each vegetable, some pickled beets, a couple of jars of plum jam and three of tomato sauce. Nacie didn't provide any bags — I think you were expected to bring your own — but she sold crocheted cotton ones. Crocheted by her, we found out. A clever way to make a few more bucks, I thought, but also decent. These old people lived clean.

"Would be good to stop using plastic bags," I said to Mom. "Producing them is real polluting and incinerating them a huge source of dioxins."

Nacie smiled at me. "Is that so?"

I nodded and smiled back.

"Okay," said Mom, and she bought every last crocheted bag, twenty some in all.

Nacie picked up one of the little pillows and slipped it into a bag.

"For you," she said to Mom.

"Thanks," said Mom without asking what the hell it was for. She started down to the car.

I looked at Nacie and was about to ask myself when she said, "It's a sleep pillow, made of lavender and flax seeds, to lay over the eyes at night. The flax has a cooling effect and the lavender calms, helps you sleep."

I nodded. "Thanks." If anyone needed sleep it was my mother.

In the car, my knee still hurt. I pulled up my pant leg to see a purple and yellow bruise starting.

By the time we got home, Mom was exhausted and went right to bed. I made her take the sleep pillow, told her how to use it. Dad helped me put the groceries away but kept making these stupid comments.

"Goat's milk, huh? Don't goats eat tin cans?"

He picked up the new shampoo. It was a leafy-green color. Organics was the name, the label claiming seventy percent organic ingredients.

"It's the other thirty percent you have worry about," said Dad.

"I doubt it," I said.

"Let me guess. Costs twice as much as regular shampoo."

As I stuffed the shopping bags under the sink, I saw two Slurpee cups in the garbage. Dad must have taken Maggie when we were out. The amount of food coloring in that shit!

Just to prove Dad wrong about the shampoo and tell him so, I looked Organics up on the net.

Turned out it had just as much chemical crap as normal shampoo. Piss me off. Using the name Organics. Didn't anyone have any morals anymore? Or was Dad right that these small amounts weren't a big deal? But then what about the billion people flushing these chemicals down the drain into streams, lakes and the feckin' ocean. And what happened when they got mixed up with chemicals in bleach, detergents, turpentine and whatever else was going down our drains? The fish bathed in it, we ate the fish... man, this world was messed.

Just to screw myself even more, I looked up babies, breast milk and carcinogens.

A newborn baby in America has 230 industrial chemicals in its blood and urine the morning it's born — 190 of which are linked to cancer.

Jeez! I punched off the computer screen. I needed to go find Davis and nuke some brain cells. No doubt dope was grown with killer pesticides 'cause the bikers and gangs who grew it wouldn't give a crap. But I refused to think about that.

Davis's line was busy so I grabbed my camera and went over there.

10 Spermbags

Davis lived with his dad because his mom traveled so much, teaching yoga at various "voodoo centers," as his dad called them. Yoga was what she got into after being married to Davis's dad. "Her detox," Davis called it.

In his room, Davis was sprinkling leaf onto some papers.

"Look in there," he said, pointing to his desk.

"Why?"

"Just look. Side cabinet." His eyebrows did a little dance.

I opened the cabinet door and was literally blinded by the light. A hole had been hacked into the cabinet's back wall, and a lamp set in the hole was shining on a half dozen little plants.

"Grow light," he explained. "Gray, meet my girls."

"Are you kidding me?" I shook my head.

"Well, I hope they're girls because the females are the only ones that produce bud. And I'm going organic with them, you'll be happy to know. They're grown with love, organic compost, and some of this stuff." He picked up a little plastic bottle. African violet plant food.

"They go nuts for this stuff. Makes them sing and do the hula."

"What do you do when they outgrow your desk?"

"Plant them."

"Where?"

"Dunno yet."

"Your dad wants you, Davis," called Laurie, rapping on the door.

"Dad's slave," whispered Davis, hooking his thumb at the door. Laurie was stepmom number two. Mom Two, as Davis called her. There was Mom One, and his actual mom who he called Real Mom.

Davis's dad met Laurie at an AA meeting. Davis said the only reason his dad had gone to the meetings was that he'd heard it was an easy place to meet women because they were all vulnerable with shame.

"One minute," called Davis, licking the rolling papers.

"Now," called back his dad.

"He wants to show you something with the fish," said Laurie anxiously.

Davis pulled the joint through his lips and slipped it in his jacket pocket. "He got a fresh salmon off a buddy who's a commercial fisherman. He's all proud. Thinks he caught it himself."

* * *

Davis's dad stood over the sink, a bloodied knife in one hand, a beer in the other.

"Come here, Dave. You, too, Gray," he ordered.

"Go see," urged Laurie.

There was a crucifix over the sink, a large cheesy pink thing that must have been new because it was too big for me to have not noticed before.

"I sliced her belly and look at this." He lifted up two herring – one looked fresh, the other half digested. "Girl's full of fish," he laughed. "Feed them to the cat." He dangled the herring over his shoulder for Laurie.

"Do you think raw fish is good for – "

"It's a cat, isn't it?"

Laurie took the slimy fish.

"And would you look at this." He dug with his knife and sniggered. "She's not a she after all. Know how you tell a girl fish from a boy fish?" He looked right at me.

"No. How?"

He lifted out some weird stringy thing with a little pouch in its center.

"Know what this is?" He leaned toward me. His breath was a tangy mix of beer and nicotine.

"No," said Davis, sounding bored.

"It's a sperm bag. A delicacy in Japan."

"Cool," said Davis unconvincingly.

"Cool," I echoed with more enthusiasm.

"You bet it's cool," said Davis's dad as he shoved Davis hard with his elbow. Davis fell against me and I hit my back on the counter. "It's cool because you didn't know it before and now you do. So your little brain learned something today. Now get out of here."

"Sorry my dad's both a creep and an asshole," said Davis once we were outside.

"What? Come on. Spermbag's a seriously dice word," I said, happy to get him to laugh. "Mine's an asshole lately, too." Though I had to admit that Davis's dad made mine look like Jesus.

* * *

Davis and I got high and took pictures. Maybe it was because the sky was an overcast, metallic gray but, unlike at that farm, everything here in the burbs looked sad. I took pictures of rusted tacks pinning yellowed paper to the dead telephone pole. Another of the cracked, crumbling sidewalk. Of mud-splattered candy wrappers in the gutters. Of the paint store sign with the neon letter T burned out so it read "Hammond's Pain."

Davis accidentally stepped on the back end of an ant and I took a close-up of its front legs clawing the air. When I swore I heard it crying, I put it out of its misery.

We walked through the playground where the red paint was chipping off the poles of the swing set. That's when I had one of those stoner realizations that seem really profound at the time.

Everything, from the moment it was made, began dying. Something was brand new for only a second of time and then it started to break down. From the tallest buildings to the smallest ant, everything was falling to pieces attempting to get back to its origins: nothing.

I thought about my body and how one day it, too, would be nothing but bone which would turn to ash which would be blown apart by the wind. Poof.

And then I started to feel faint and had to sit down on one of the swings.

"Hey," said Davis, taking the swing next to me. "Here's one. Every night before the bogeyman goes to sleep, he checks under his bed for Chuck Norris." He laughed his donkey guffaw and I started laughing, too. Then, as if some switch was broken inside, I couldn't stop. I laughed till my head felt like it was spinning and then I started having trouble breathing so had to calm myself down.

"You know those little signs in the school stairwell?" I said when I could breathe again. I was feeling all serious now. "The ones that say don't disturb or remove?"

"Sure."

"Those walls are full of asbestos."

"Yeah?" Davis started to pump his swing.

"That shit is like one of the most carcinogenic substances in existence."

"But don't you like have to inhale it?" Davis said as he swung by, his voice loud then soft.

"I don't know. Still."

Davis was swinging seriously high now and singing some song I couldn't make out.

"I thought you could trust adults," I said. "But maybe they're not smart. Maybe they're idiots. And we're being taught to be idiots, too – to go to school, get an education, then a job so we can buy a killer car, then a toxic house full of toxic crap, buy new improved lemon-scented detergent that kills the ocean..."

Davis was swinging really high now.

"You know what?" I said.

Davis launched into the air, ridiculously high, and landed on his feet in the sand with a dull smack.

"What?" He jumped around to face me, chest out, hands on his hips like a superhero.

"I'm going to quit my stupid job."

"Yeah, stupid job. Although, I'll miss those free previews."

"I want go live like a caveman."

"Oo-oo, ya," yelled Davis, nodding. He stabbed a finger toward me. "Goo, ma, moo?" He hunched up his shoulders and began pretend-picking his nose. He spoke in grunts and gestures the rest of the night, and I understood every word.

* * *

When I got home, it was way past my curfew. Normally Mom would have gotten out of bed to throw a mild fit but she didn't bother. She wasn't sweating the small stuff, I guess.

Maggie was passed out on the couch in the living room, her movie still playing on the TV. I turned it off. Every so often her pain was so uncomfortable, she couldn't sleep and ended up down here zoning out on TV. She was all set up with pillows and comforter. On the coffee table was an apple core and half-eaten rice cake spread with almond butter, a glass of water, a box of unbleached tissues, two prescription bottles and a deck of cards. She and Mom had an ongoing rummy match, a penny a point.

Snoring through her nose, Maggie was making little pig

snuffles. In the old days, meaning a few weeks ago, I would have pinched her nostrils closed, laughed as she struggled to catch a breath and then startled awake.

Asleep, she looked even younger than twelve. More like a perfectly healthy six-year-old. She was holding a bottle of pink nail polish in one hand, her nails a pearly pink. I pulled out my camera and snapped some pictures.

A raised voice came from upstairs. I couldn't tell whose, but it didn't sound happy.

In the kitchen I grabbed a bag of baked not fried potato chips, a couple of organic bananas and a glass of goat's milk and went downstairs. I sipped the milk. It was thicker than I was used to and had a goaty thing going on but it wasn't bad.

I went online and looked up nail polish. Nail polish contained phthalates, a carcinogen. Shit. Maybe it was the nail polish. Maggie loved painting her nails. Had been doing it since she was three. I'd tell Mom tomorrow.

I would have thought Dad would know this stuff. He was the scientist in the family, after all.

I watched some TV, then went on line and messaged Nat.

looking forward 2 Friday. killer fettucini alfredo at Little Italy? caesar salad, garlic bread, tiramisu.

If she couldn't decide where to go, I might as well. I hoped I spelled the dessert thing right. Dad took us there on Mother's Day last year and I got that very dinner. It was seriously good.

looking 4ward 2 ur place after.

I got all warm thinking about those condoms in my wallet. Those spermbags, I thought, and burst out laughing. Just like at the playground, laughter took me over like some sort of internal earthquake, and I almost puked my goat's milk.

I thought to warn Nat about the crap that was in her whitening toothpaste. I was about to sign off and go masturbate my way into oblivion when a message popped up.

It was Ciel.

hi gray, how's maggie feeling? it must be so hard for your folks. and what about u? r u doing alright?

I suddenly choked up and couldn't write back. Since Maggie's diagnosis, not one person had asked how I was doing.

* * *

Monday morning at school, I ran into Natalie and company by the Coke machine. The benzene machine as I thought of it, which was next to the hydrogenated fat machine full of chips and candy bars.

Erin, her eyes bright and nervous, asked how my mom was doing.

"She's okay," I shrugged and checked out Nat's new hair. "Whoa, your hair looks amazing." A matching midnight blue bra strap showed at her shoulder. A new bra. Just for me?

Nat smiled her bleached white smile, tossed her hair from her eyes but didn't answer me back.

"My mom and I saw your mom in the grocery store on Saturday," said Erin, glancing at Natalie. "She was like yelling at the manager. And she had a cart full of groceries but she wasn't buying them, she was returning them."

"Yeah, well. It's because of Maggie. We're trying to clean out all the chemicals from – "

"I thought she was going to hit him," said Erin.

The bell rang and the girls scuttled off down the hall, taking Natalie with them.

I looked for Natalie between classes as well as at lunch but our paths somehow didn't cross. After school I saw her driving off with her mom. She hadn't said a word to me all day.

Later, I tried to call her. Her mother answered and told me she was out.

"Can you ask her to call me?"

"Sure, sweetie. Though I know she has a lot of homework to catch up on."

Natalie didn't call back, but then Mom had been talking to Grammy on the phone most of the night so I didn't think anything of it.

* * *

The next day I found her alone by her locker and slipped my arm around her beautiful waist. She startled.

"Oh, you scared me, Gray. Don't," she said and took a step away.

Don't what? "Hey, I made reservations at Little Italy."

She nodded. "Yeah, you told me."

"Can't wait," I said and paused, hoping she'd say the same. When she didn't, I asked if she wanted to get a slice at lunch despite the fact that I'd brought my lunch – homemade squash muffins and kale soup – in solidarity with Maggie.

"I have to spend lunch in the library. English stuff." She took hold of the sleeve of my red shirt and rubbed it between her fingers. "Nice color. What's this scratchy material? Raw silk?"

"Organic hemp. Found out that growing cotton uses – "

"Really?" she laughed. "A marijuana shirt?"

"Not quite the same kind of hemp."

"Why did you send me that stuff about my toothpaste?"

"Well, because it's got a lot of toxic crap in it."

"Probably why it works so well." She huffed a little laugh. "Anyway, I gotta go."

I suddenly wanted to run after her, grab her, hold her, kiss her, make her want me as much as I wanted her.

Desperation, I reminded myself, was not cool. So me and my organic shirt walked away.

11   Matter Minds

Maggie was in the kitchen eating her organic porridge, Mom at the counter kneading dough. She'd started making her own bread. Maggie was wearing a new shirt. I was starting to notice things like that.

"Hey, Maggie, new shirt?"

"I silkscreened one of those organic cotton T-shirts Mom got…" She leaned back real slow in her chair as if it hurt to do so and stretched the navy blue surface flat. "It's the moon, see, surrounded by stars." She pointed out a scatter of little silver bits. "And this hazy swirl up here is the Milky Way."

"Isn't it great?" said Mom a little too enthusiastically. "Designed it herself."

"Yeah, it's good." I grabbed an apple and the phone rang.

"Can you drive me to school?" Maggie asked Mom. "My legs are achy and – "

"Of course I'll drive you. And I'll pick you up," she said and answered the phone.

Maggie left to go brush her teeth. I ate my apple and listened to Mom.

"Yes, I know. That shouldn't be a problem." She laughed lightly. "It's been like a circus around here but I should have them ready by then, yes."

Must be the bank banners. I couldn't remember the last time I'd seen Mom in her studio. Actually, I could. It was the day we got that phone call with the results of Maggie's test. Since then she'd spent all her time reading about cancer and cooking.

"I can take Mag on the back of my bike and pick her up," I said when she got off the phone.

"You get out at different times and I don't want her on the back of your bike, thank you."

"For all we know, car spew is at the root of Maggie's – "

Mom closed her eyes and held her hand up like a stop sign.

"I can't hear that right now, Gray," she said. "I just can't. Sorry."

Fine, I thought. Be like Dad. I knew he'd bought Maggie a Big Mac the other day because I smelled it on her breath. Jerk.

*　*　*

When I got home from school, Maggie was in the living room propped up on the couch under her comforter and writing on a clipboard. I noticed a bump pushing up under the skin on her arm just below her bent elbow. A tumor?

"Hey, look at my Love rice." She pointed at the jar. I guess it hurt too much to reach for it. "The Love jar still hasn't got any mold. Cool, eh? But it's starting to turn yellow. I don't know what that means yet." Her voice sounded wheezy, like she was all stuffed up. She rubbed the side of her nose. "The other two jars are pretty moldy now. But the ignored jar still has more mold than the Hate jar."

After all Mom and I had done, Maggie still seemed to be getting worse. I guess we weren't doing enough. Or maybe Maggie wasn't doing enough.

"Dr. Emoto says it's the water in the rice that's affected by our thoughts and intentions. Water takes impressions of everything." She scrunched her nose and rubbed her face again. "He says it has great memory."

"You know, Mag, eating crap food like Big Macs is not doing yourself any good."

"I just had one," she said defensively. "Julie's mom took us through the drive-through. Quit bugging me about it." She turned away from me.

Okay, so it wasn't Dad this time. "It's your – " I was about to say funeral but stopped myself. I sighed. "Yeah, sorry. So your project almost finished?"

Her three-paneled posterboard had MATTER MINDS pasted across the top in blue letters. The letters were jaggedly outlined with one of Dad's neon yellow highlighters to make it look as though they were vibrating. On the coffee table were scattered photographs of the rice jars in their various stages.

"Dad's got to photocopy some pictures from the book," she said without looking at me, "and I still have stuff to figure out before I write my report."

I started to leave, wondered if there were any muffins around.

As I turned the corner into the hall I heard behind me, "I'm bleeding."

"What?" I backed up. Maggie's nose was running like a faucet onto her comforter.

"Mom!" I didn't have a clue where she was. "Maggie needs you. Now." It's just a nosebleed, I told myself, calm down. I ran to the kitchen and grabbed the roll of paper towels.

Mom met me in the living room.

"It's just a nose bleed," I said, though the amount of blood streaming out was ridiculous.

"Pinch the bridge, Maggie," said Mom.

"My new shirt," Maggie whined.

"It'll wash out. Just lie back."

Maggie lay back and instantly started choking. Sitting back up she began to cough blood.

That wasn't right. Blood shouldn't come out of your mouth.

"Get the ice pack, Gray – and a bowl." Mom's voice was shaking.

"Sure." I was happy to get out of there.

Mom applied ice and Maggie pinched. Nothing dulled the bright red flow into the bowl. Mom called the oncologist's office, asked what she should do.

"I'm taking her to emergency," she said after she hung up. "Maggie, we have to change your shirt. Then, Gray, you help me get her into the car." She spoke with a weird forced calm but her eyes were wild, her movements kind of spastic.

"Yeah, sure, Mom."

"It's going to be fine. You're all right, Maggie. Don't worry. It's just a nosebleed. It's going to be fine. You're going to be fine."

Behind her bloody washcloth, Maggie did look like the calmest person around. Maybe it was the drugs.

I practically had to carry her to the car, she was so weak, Mom trotting alongside holding the bowl under Maggie's leaky nose as she reminded me three times to call Dad.

"Tell him to shop for dinner on his way home. And will you throw Maggie's comforter and shirt in the wash? Cold water, remember. Cold water."

I watched them drive away, the car spewing carcinogens all the way to the hospital. Before they turned the corner, Mom swerved after nearly hitting a parked car.

Shit. Calm down, I thought, as they drove out of sight.

I collected the bloodied stuff – God, there was a lot of blood – and threw them in the washer.

Now I had to call Dad who I was trying to avoid these days. Which wasn't hard because he was putting in extra long hours at work, and when he was home, he spent his time with Maggie, not me. But I did as Mom asked, called and told him what was happening and told him about dinner. He didn't ask for details, just said okay. He sounded like a feckin' robot.

* * *

He arrived home with ground beef and hamburger buns.

"Vegetarian beef?" I said.

"Free-range," he said. "No steroidal hormones, no antibiotics."

"No dioxins?"

"You don't have to eat it." He slapped a pack of tofu burgers on the counter. "I bought these, too. I happen to want some meat."

"You're going to tempt Maggie. And Mom'll be pissed."

"Lucky for you, you don't make the rules around here," he said with a stern stare. "Now would you cut some red onions, please?"

Spermbag, I thought, picking up an onion.

He made up the patties and threw one into the pan. It started to sizzle, the meat smell rising, and my mouth watered like a dog.

I heard Mom come in the front door.

Dad took a breath as if steeling himself before going into the foyer. I followed. He and Mom barely looked at each other, just exchanged a few quiet words before Dad went outside to carry a sleeping Maggie from the car. In his arms, she looked smaller than normal. Her face was really pale.

"Don't bump her legs," whispered Mom as he started upstairs.

"Gray, go flip the burgers, please," said Dad.

I went back to the kitchen. Mom came in and plopped down silently into a chair. The air reeked of frying beef but she didn't even mention it. I flipped the burgers, then started slicing a tomato.

"The bleeding stopped," was all she said. She talked like she was in some kind of trance. "It was from a tumor."

My appetite dived south.

"In the sinus cavity. It's putting pressure on her face."

"That sucks." My knife slipped, cutting my finger. More blood. Normally I would announce my cut to the world, asked for a Band-Aid at least, and Mom would give me one of her worried-mom looks. That look alone always made me feel better. But now her face was permanently worried, and she didn't need my stupid little cut to add to it.

I felt the pain rise a minute after the blood. My head seemed to pinch up to a point before the ache settled into an even throb. It wasn't very deep and I knew it would stop hurting after five minutes.

"The oncologist at the hospital guesses she has six months."

"Six months?" I repeated dumbly.

"At best."

Mom had been given different time frames from different doctors – a year, one to two years, and the optimistic "people can do surprising things." Today's guess was the shortest prediction yet.

I counted off in my head. April, May, June, July, August, September. I wondered if Maggie would make it to her birthday: August 30. If she'd ever be a teen.

"I have to go for a walk," blurted Mom, nodding real fast. "I have to walk."

She had dark circles under her eyes. The last thing she looked like she needed was exercise.

"Don't you want to have a veggie burger first?"

"I have to walk," she said and left the room.

Since Dad was eating meat I refused to eat with him and took my dinner downstairs. He didn't say anything.

I sat in front of the TV, started flicking around. I passed two commercials for SUVs, which I'd learned polluted three times as much as an ordinary car. Saw another for cancerous pop, another for cancerous shampoo and conditioner, another for beer. Alcohol was on the cancer list, too.

Did the world have some sort of feckin' death wish?

The phone rang and, just to spite Dad, I didn't answer it.

"Gray, it's for you," Dad called downstairs.

I picked up and heard him hang up the other phone.

"Gray?" It was Natalie.

"Hi, thank God you called. Man, my dad is driving me – "

"I want to break up, Gray."

"You want to – "

"I just don't think we're really right for each other."

I stood up, lifting the coffee table off its legs, my burger flipping to the floor.

"You mean because my sister has some deadly disease, my mother shops in reverse and I wear marijuana shirts."

Natalie paused. "No, no. It's just time, I think."

"It's just time? Two days before…" It was shallow of me, sure, but she could have at least waited until after I lost my V-card.

"It's just how I feel…"

I looked at the gold-ribboned box on my desk, thought of those two stolen condoms in my wallet, the reservation I'd made at Little Italy.

"Fine, if that's how you feel."

"Yeah, sorry." She almost sounded sad until she chirped, "Still friends, I hope?"

I heaved the plastic petroleum phone across the room. It made a serious dent in the drywall, and I imagined a cloud of formaldehyde bursting forth.

12 Breakup and Breakdown

Friday night, and instead of sitting across from my first lay and eating great Italian food, I was at home eating with my asshole dad, freaked-out mom and ill sister.

I hadn't gone to school, had told Mom I wasn't feeling well. She'd panicked at first until I told her I felt fine and just needed a day off. I didn't want to have to pass Natalie's breasts in the hall, see her friends stare.

I got Davis to skip, too, and we spent the day at his place, playing music we were convinced would stimulate plant growth and trash-talking Natalie. Davis, who'd never liked Natalie, called her all the names he always wanted to call her but didn't because of me: Brainless Slut Bucket, Boobs for Brains, Jerk-around Dickface, etc.

Mom had made a stir-fry of onions and garlic, chard and carrot plus little chalk-white squares of tofu. This mix was humped over brown rice. The chard was kind of bitter and the onions a little hard. The tofu seemed to have no taste other than the organic tamari sauce I dumped over it, but I wasn't going to complain. That was Dad's job.

Maggie begged for ketchup and Mom finally gave it to her.

Dad took a long sip from the glass of wine he'd poured for himself. He wasn't a drinker, would have a couple of glasses at a party or a beer or two on Saturday night in front of the game. Having wine with dinner on a weekday was some sort of statement.

"Curious meal," he said.

Knew it, I thought smugly.

Mom shot him a look. "It's macrobiotic. A very well-known and ancient healing diet. I know it seems a little spare but I believe it's the way to go."

"It tastes good for you." I was trying to say something nice without lying.

"You don't have to do this just for me," said Maggie, the corner of her mouth smudged with ketchup.

"Yes, yes, we do," said Mom. "And it's not just for you but for us, too. For everyone, actually. Everyone everywhere." Mom glanced hard at Dad, as if challenging him to contradict her.

Dad stepped right up to the plate. "We can still practice moderation and try to enjoy ourselves a little."

Mom's shoulders seemed to grow epaulets. Dad sipped his wine.

"The rice is nice and chewy," I said.

Mom forced a smile and turned to Maggie.

"I was thinking about your birthday, Maggie. Becoming a teenager and all, I thought a big party was in order this year. We could hire Dr. Fry the Science Guy?"

"That would be great," said Maggie.

Dr. Fry was a local magician/scientist we'd seen perform at a fundraiser for the university's new biotech wing.

"Make sure he brings the pinwheel," I said. Dr. Fry did optical illusion stuff. For example, he'd ask the audience to stare at this moving pinwheel for three minutes and then at his head and his head would slowly expand to twice its normal size. It was sick.

"And how about getting the bug zoo to come with some specimens?" continued Mom.

"Wow," said Maggie.

Maggie's birthday was months away. But Mom had also been reading about positive attitudes and healing. Having projects and things to look forward to apparently boosted the immune system. Which was why she wanted Maggie to keep up with her homework.

"I bet they'd do such a thing. Don't you, Ethan?" said Mom.

"If you pay people enough money, they'll do anything," said Dad. He was refilling his wine glass. Had barely touched his tofu.

Mom changed the subject and asked Maggie how her project was coming along.

"You know how the Love rice was turning that weird yellow? Well, Dad said it's started fermenting!" she said happily.

"Seems to be turning into rice wine," said Dad, toasting to it.

"I'm writing in my report that the rice is drunk on

love." Maggie laughed, which seemed to make her cough.

"Alcohol's on the American Cancer Society's list of carcinogens," I said, looking at Dad.

"Good thing I don't drink," said Maggie.

We all burst out laughing, even Mom, tears rimming her eyes.

* * *

After dinner, and despite the fact that it was raining out, Mom left the dishes to Dad and me and went for a walk. She used to work in her studio after dinner. Now she walked in great big circles around the school playing field. Every night for like an hour. I could see her through the glass doors to the deck, weaving in and out of trees, hooded, hunched slightly forward.

If I could see her, the neighbors could, too.

Dad did the dishes and I cleared the table. Clearing and scraping dishes had become my job now that Maggie had to lie down after dinner.

"We should be having feasts every night," said Dad. "All of Maggie's favorite foods."

"But don't you think it's worth trying stuff to cure it?"

"It's not going to cure it," he said with a slow blink. "No macrobiotic diet, no turmeric pills, no organic shampoo is going to make any — "

"Well, maybe it'll slow it down at least."

"I wish I could believe that," he said, implying he was smart and I wasn't.

I stopped, ketchup in hand. "Why are you so goddamn pessimistic?"

Dad stopped then, too, and held up a threatening finger. "Don't you talk to me that way."

"Spermbag," I muttered and stuck the ketchup in the fridge.

"What did you say?" Dad came and stood on the other side of the fridge door.

"Nothing." I shut the fridge and there we were, face to face.

Between being dumped by Natalie and listening to his negative shit, I'd had it. My muscles involuntarily flexed. I was as tall as him now. Didn't have his bulk but bet I could take him.

Dad shook his head as if he was real disappointed in me. He turned and went back to the dishes.

But I was the one who was disappointed. Mr. Scientist was the one with zero ideas and zero answers. Who wasn't even trying to help.

I left, not bothering to finish clearing the table and went downstairs. I waited for him to yell at me to come back and finish the job.

But he didn't.

* * *

Saturday, first day of March Break. Needless to say we weren't going skiing. Not that I wanted to. Not with my family anyway.

The Russian agents came as usual, Dasha armed with her aerosols. Mom had arranged the new non-toxic cleansers on the kitchen counter. I was heading out to meet Hughie and Davis at the skate park but stopped to watch her explain to the unsmiling couple what each bottle was for and the dangers to themselves and others of using chemical cleaners. Dasha was glancing sadly from the old bottles on her belt to the new ones on the counter. One dark eyebrow raised, Sergei looked as if he thought Mom was secretly trying to poison them.

When Davis, Hughie and I arrived back at my place later for some food, Mom was just pulling up in the car. The back seat was filled with groceries bulging in their crocheted bags.

"Can we help?" said Davis, who was a suck-up around other people's parents. Like he was hoping to get adopted or something.

"Thanks, Davis," said Mom. She looked thinner and her hair was graying at the temples. Maybe she dyed her hair and I never knew it, but whatever, she looked way older to me suddenly.

As we stepped inside the house, a familiar lemony cocktail stirred the air.

I looked at Mom who looked at me. Her jaw tightened and she headed straight into the living room.

Don't mess with Sergei, I wanted to say. He was mopping the living-room floor, Dasha spraying the dining table with her old lemon-scented furniture polish.

"What are you doing?" Mom yelled, waving her arms.

Dasha turned her sad eyes on Mom. "The new spray did not work so well."

"I have a sick daughter upstairs!" Mom grabbed the can right out of Dasha's hand and shook it in front of her face.

Sergei had stopped mopping. "This stuff makes people sick. I will not have it used in my house."

"Whoa," said Hughie beside me, glancing sideways at Davis.

"Why don't you guys go downstairs?" I said, embarrassed they were witnessing my mom losing it. "I'll be there in a minute."

Sergei had come up behind Mom and now he snatched back the spray can. Mom turned on him. I thought I was going to have to heave my crocheted net bags across the room, but he calmly announced, "We are leaving now. Come, Dasha." They gathered up their mop, buckets, broom and toxic cleansers and left, Sergei's bucket knocking my bruised knee on their way out.

I shut the door behind them, relieved to see them go.

"Whoa, Mom. You didn't have to go ballistic on them."

She whipped her face toward me. "Don't tell me how I'm supposed to feel and act. Okay?"

"Sorry, I just thought you could have – "

"Don't ever tell me," she repeated, her voice like a coiled spring, "how I'm supposed to feel and act."

I backed off, went to put the groceries in the kitchen. I thought Mom and I were on the same team here, but maybe I was wrong.

"I have to walk," Mom announced and left, leaving the front door open behind her, cold air streaming in.

I shut the door for the second time, then went upstairs to check on Maggie in case she'd heard Mom yelling.

She was asleep, a fat Harry Potter book face down on

her chest. She looked even more pale than usual. Holding my breath, I went closer, stared at the book to make sure it was rising and falling with her breath. It was. I laughed at myself, but moved the book off her chest anyway, because it looked so heavy.

Downstairs, Davis asked in a quiet voice if my mom was all right.

I shrugged. "Yeah, she's okay. Went for a walk."

"She needs to seriously chill," said Hughie. "That was nuts." He screwed up his face. "She's worried about furniture spray?"

I turned on him. "Yes, Hughie, she is. And so am I. And if you weren't so ignorant, you'd know that your stinky antiperspirant has at least three carcinogens in it not to mention aluminum which causes dementia which is probably why you're so feckin' stupid. And that the eighty different chemicals in your hair gel – "

"You're even more psycho than your mother," said Hughie, moving toward the door.

"Screw you, Hughie."

"You screw you," he shot back. He opened the door. "You know, you're boring as shit now," he said and left, leaving the door open behind him.

"Close the door," I yelled. And when he didn't, I slammed it shut.

*   *   *

That night I was supposed to work at the Cineplex. Instead, uniform in hand, I walked into the manager's office and told him, "I quit."

"We need two weeks' notice, Gray. You know that."

"So sue me." Then I listed off the carcinogens in the food they sold. "I'm not selling cancer." I dropped my uniform on his desk and walked out of there.

I, for one, was going to stop being a hypocrite.

13 Drop Out

At breakfast, I told Mom I'd quit my job and was also quitting school. She was making some macrobiotic casserole that smelled suspiciously like vomit.

"You quit your job? And what's this about school?" She stopped chopping onions, looked at me as if she hadn't heard right.

Dad came in to get his coffee.

"I can drive Mag this morning," he said without looking at either me or Mom.

"Fine, but Gray here has decided he's quitting school?" said Mom. "Is that right?"

"You got it."

Dad did look at me now, eyes flashing. "What are you talking about?"

"I'm not going back until they take the asbestos insulation out of the walls. And the benzene machines and the transfat machines. I mean, why am I going to a school that sets that sort of example? What am I supposed to be learning from that?" I'd had my little speech ready.

"First of all," began Mr. Scientist, "it's safer to leave asbestos where it is than remove it — "

"I don't believe that," I said. "I don't believe anything you say anymore."

Dad threw up his hands. "I think I liked it better when you spoke in single-word sentences."

I gave him the finger only didn't raise my hand.

"I'm going to work," he said, filling his travel mug. "And if you're quitting school, Gray, just know that you will not be living here rent free."

"Ethan," began Mom.

"You either go to school or you get a full-time job. That's my rule."

"Exactly what I was thinking," I said smugly.

"Good," said Dad. "I'll decide what to charge you for room and board." He took his coffee out the door.

"Gray, let's you and me talk about this," said Mom.

"There's nothing to talk about. I'm going to stop being part of the problem."

* * *

I misjudged the distance to Happy Valley farm, and it took me over an hour to get there. The produce stand was empty and I pushed my bike up the path toward the house. There had been a shitload of hills on the way over and my legs were insanely tired.

I leaned my bike against a tree, scanned for that attack rooster and walked up the steps to the veranda. I knocked and inside, a dog went off like a truck horn.

The woman, Nacie, came to the door. She was shorter

than I remembered, same mismatched eyes. I introduced myself, said that my mom shopped here twice a week.

"I know your mother and I remember you, Gray," she said.

"And I remember seeing your Help Wanted sign. I'd like to work for you."

"Oh?" She looked at me. "How old are you?"

"Seventeen," I lied.

"Who is it, Nace?" came a gruff voice from inside. This was followed by a huge woof that echoed in my chest.

"Why don't you come in and we'll talk. We're just having lunch." She smiled. It was a smug kind of smile, as if she had a secret. I only hoped it wasn't something twisted.

The house was old. Wood floors. No carpets. I even think the walls were plaster, not drywall.

These people were doing it right, I thought as I followed her to the kitchen.

I stopped in the doorway.

"Whoa," I said aloud. Ten feet away, the biggest dog in the world was baring his black gums and two-inch teeth at me.

"Not to worry. Litze's just smiling at you."

"Oh?"

Up close, this dog looked seriously mixed up. It had long flap ears like a bloodhound, a pointy collie's nose and a huge fat skull like a St. Bernard's. Its long legs were covered in shaggy hair when nothing else was. And the tail was one long pointy curl.

"Come say hi, Litze," said Nacie.

The creature instantly lowered its massive head and wagged its way over for a pat, ear flaps swaying. Correction: ear flap. One of his ears was missing, a stump of transparent pink cartilage in its place.

This was the ugliest dog I'd ever seen.

"This is Litze, Gray. Litze, this is Gray." Its shoulders came up to my waist.

"Hi, boy," I said, hoping I didn't sound afraid. I held my hand under his snout, then patted his ugly head.

"He's part Afghan and part Great Dane," she explained. "Maybe something else thrown in."

"What sort of name is Litze?" I asked.

"It's Norwegian. Means little one." She smiled her sly smile again.

Norwegian humor, I guess.

Mr. Daskaloff hadn't gotten up from the kitchen table. He had a long, slightly horsey face, broad and gently rounded shoulders.

"Milan," she said. "This is Gray Fallon. Gray, my husband, Milan."

"Mr. Daskaloff," he corrected her, extending a weathered but strong hand, the middle finger nothing but a one-inch stub.

Was everyone missing body parts on this farm?

"Nice to meet you," I said. He nodded.

"Gray wants to work on the farm." She invited me to sit down, then collected a napkin (a cloth one), spoon and knife and set them in front of me.

"You'll have some bean soup," she said.

"Thanks." I was starving, and it smelled great.

"Help yourself to a roll, butter's on the table. Pass him the rolls, Milan."

Mr. Daskaloff passed me the rolls.

"Thanks."

Nacie gave me a bowl of soup, then sat down. The soup tasted like health itself, the roll still warm and both obviously homemade.

"So, Gray," she began. "You're interested in the job."

"Yes, I've – "

"He's thin," said Mr. Daskaloff.

"He'll get stronger," said Nacie as she buttered her roll.

"Pale."

"The sun will take care of that."

"Too young."

Hello, right beside you, not deaf.

Nacie cleared her throat and turned to me. "So, Gray, maybe you could tell us what makes you want to work here." She bit into her roll.

Since I was too thin, too pale and too young, I didn't have anything to lose so I went ahead and told them about Maggie and how I believed her cancer was environmentally caused.

"You seem to live clean," I said.

"Well we live simply – "

"I want to live a life that doesn't cause cancer. People think it can't be done. Even my dad. I want to prove they're wrong."

"That's quite noble. Isn't it, Milan?" she announced as if this was great fun.

"It's very hard work," he answered, frowning.

"I can start right away. Today, tomorrow?"

Nacie was smiling.

Then I had a brilliant thought. I sat up straighter in my chair. "I was wondering…"

"Yes, Gray?" asked Nacie.

"If you don't mind, I'd really like to live in your woods."

14   Caveman

A week later, I was woken not by my clock radio playing tunes from my fave rock station but by Clarence, the demented rooster.

Clarence didn't crow. He pecked. When the sun rose in the east – luckily on the other side of the woods, which meant I got a half hour more sleep – he flew to the roof of the horse barn and tapped Morse code on the rusty weathervane (which happened to be a rooster).

Then, because a few pecks would make the weathervane move, he'd have to catch up to it. So the tapping was followed by a scrabble of his chicken feet. Tap, tap, tap, tap, tap. Scratch, scritch, scratch, scritch, scratch. Tap, tap, tap, tap, tap. Scratch, scritch, scratch, scritch, scratch. Squeak. (The old weathervane squeaked at one sticking point in the revolution.)

It was an irritating way to wake up, but effective.

I sat up in my bed – a wooden platform I'd banged together from some (untreated) scrap wood in Mr. D.'s workshed, an organic cotton futon and an old army-issue sleeping bag (one hundred percent cotton with wool batting). The sleeping bag I got from Salvation Army. The futon I bought new so it took half my savings.

This morning the outer layer of my bag was damp with dew. Even my hair felt wet. I shivered in the cool morning air. Maybe I'd grab a toque next time I was home. Through my net walls (some old cotton fishing nets I found at a flea market) a pale blue sky dawned over the valley while a giant hotdog of mist rolled along its bottom.

I thought of my steaming morning showers back home, lay back down and closed my eyes. Tap, tap, tap, tap, tap. Scratch, scritch, scratch, scritch, scratch. Squeak.

I was tired. The night sounds had been making me paranoid and keeping me awake. I didn't think there was anything really dangerous out here – Nacie said she hadn't seen a bear for five years, then corrected herself saying maybe it was two – but still, I was pretty damn exposed, my roof nothing but an old canvas tarp Mr. D. had dug up, my fishnet walls more holes than anything. I'd weighted the net walls down with rocks and trusted that was enough to keep out squirrels and raccoons and the bigger mice, meaning rats. My floor was earth. But that was okay. At least it could never get dirty.

I'd set myself up at the back of the property, at the top of the hill along the tree line. The tree canopy protected me from wind and rain, which was good because the canvas tarp wasn't waterproof. But I was determined to avoid plastics, nylons and polyesters, or anything else made from petroleum because of all the crap by-product.

A mosquito buzzed in my ear. I swatted it and ducked my head inside my bag.

Work started at seven so I forced myself out of bed and threw on my clothes.

This was my first real work week. Last week was devoted to setting up my place and being shown around the farm, told what would be expected of me and all. Like how I couldn't piss in the woods but had to use their old ramshackle outhouse where the toilet seat froze your ass off. How Nacie would provide lunch but I was responsible for my own breakfast and dinner. I was allowed all the chicken eggs I could eat and free access to their produce but any other food I'd have to buy. I was to get paid twenty-five a week, which would more or less cover my food and extra things like soap.

I also had free access to wild food. Dad, as a joke, had given me a book called *Living Wild.* It was actually proving handy. The mushroom section especially. I loved mushrooms and the book clearly showed how to tell the edible ones from the ones that would cause people's faces to melt before your eyes, or make your brain implode.

Mom was pretty freaked about me doing this and made me promise to come home every weekend. Which was kind of ruining the point but since I couldn't very well abandon Maggie, I agreed as long as I wasn't charged rent. Mom promised she'd work that out with Dad. Maggie thought what I was doing was cool and as soon as the weather got a bit warmer and I had my food thing down, I told her she could come visit. Be great to get her out of the polluted city, out of the offgassing house. A kind of detox.

I put my hiking boots on and went to collect mush-rooms from the woods, some scallions from the garden and a few stray lamb's-quarters — weeds, but all right tast-ing and, so my book said, the highest source of calcium of any green thing you could eat.

Keeping one eye out for Clarence, I went to hunt eggs. Clarence, the watchcock, didn't like people touching his hens' eggs. Though the dozen chickens usually slept in the coop, they ran free during the day and therefore hid their eggs all over the farm. It was like a big Easter egg hunt.

I discovered a nest of three in the tall grass not far from my tent. Just as I bent to pick them up, Clarence came shooting out from behind my tent. I jumped, screeched like a girl, then ran at him, flapping my arms. Nacie had told me just to "show him who's the bigger chicken." Clarence fled, glaring at me over his shoulder.

I had picked up a used hotplate and Nacie had lent me three extension cords which I plugged into an outlet in Mr. D.'s workshed. He was not too happy about my leaching off their electricity and neither was I, so over the weekend I'd written a solar power company asking for a donation of some solar panels and a generator. In the letter I'd tried to make myself sound like a noble cause. Played the sick sister card.

I fried up my veggies and eggs in some organic butter I kept in a metal (not plastic) cooler in a hole I'd dug into the ground. I dug up one of Nacie's buns saved from yester-day's lunch. Then, sitting on this stump that I'd hauled out of the woods, I ate while I watched that hotdog of mist slowly evaporate into the warming air.

* * *

My first job of the day was to turn and water the compost – three giant bins of it – using a pitchfork. Mr. D. showed me how he wanted it done. He stabbed a giant forkful of the stuff – leaves and grass mixed with dirt and food scraps – and flipped it in the air into an empty fourth bin. This third bin was to be flipped into the fourth, the second into the third, etc. Then next week the process would be reversed.

He did a few more forkfuls, then handed me the pitchfork.

When I tried to copy him, I was shocked at how heavy it was. I could lift maybe half the amount he had. I thought I heard him sigh. So I was left to the job, mixing in dirt and water between every dozen forkfuls.

After ten minutes my arm muscles burned. Every fifteen minutes I had to sit down and rest. After an hour I thought my back would break.

It made me realize that Mr. D., who had to be sixty-something, could probably beat me up. A sad and therefore motivating thought.

After I'd turned the last bin and watered it, I helped Nacie plant some peas and green beans. That I could handle.

Odd as she was, Nacie was good company, and she told me lots of stuff about gardening. How planting marigolds kept pests away and how slugs wouldn't cross a moat of ash or how weevils would take shelter from the morning sun in a rolled-up newspaper.

She left me to dig a slug moat around the garden while she made lunch. An hour later, when the sun hit the top of the sky, her brass bell rang out.

Today it was Bulgarian potato dumplings – Mr. D.'s mother's recipe – cold beet and fennel salad, and these excellent-looking sausage patties. I hadn't eaten meat for a month and I hadn't worked this physically hard ever. My body was screaming for those sausage patties but I said I wasn't eating meat and took a pass. Mr. D. gave me a weird look and Nacie asked if I was vegetarian. I said yes, kind of, and launched into my dioxin speech and mentioned hormones and antibiotics in animal feed.

"I see," said Nacie. "I can't say about that dioxin thing but we get our meat from Mr. Keefer up the road. He doesn't feed his pigs any drugs or strange things. Though he does dress them up sometimes." She didn't elaborate.

"Well, maybe just one," I said.

The patties were so good I ended up eating three more. Then, realizing they used an old cast-iron stove for cooking as well as heating, I felt it my duty to mention that burning wood released PAHs into the atmosphere.

"And what are these PAHs?" asked Nacie.

I'd forgotten what the letters stood for.

"I don't really know the science behind them but they're considered carcinogenic."

Mr. D. frowned at me and Nacie just nodded.

"Is that a fact?" she said. "We've been doing things a certain way for so long, we've never thought of that, have we, Milan?"

Milan grumbled something I didn't catch and Nacie offered me some brownies.

* * *

That afternoon, Mr. D. gave me the revolting job of mucking chicken crap out of the chicken coop. The smell alone was enough to make me almost toss my patties. I think he was trying to scare me and my makeshift house the hell off his property. Which only made me more determined.

Outside Clarence was running in circles and pecking at the coop walls, insanely pissed that I was in his house. I didn't dare take my eyes off the door in case he flew in and pecked my eyes out. Every so often I'd see his head in the doorway and I'd screech and toss chicken crap at him. Mr. D. kept checking back to see if I was doing a good enough job: getting under the roosts, mucking out the corners, the cobwebs, etc. I worked my butt off and by the end of the day, four-thirty, was sore where I didn't even know I had muscles.

I dragged myself up the hill to my tent. There was a dead mouse on the path. A neighbor's cat must have got it because an owl or hawk would have eaten it. It was lying on its side, so plump and fresh looking it could have been sleeping if it weren't for the blood around its nose and mouth.

The blood made me think of Maggie, and as a fly came and landed on its staring eye, I nudged it into the long grass with the toe of my hiking boot.

I was thirsty as hell, but the two glass jugs Nacie had given me were both empty. I dragged myself back down the hill to the outdoor tap. The farm used well water, no chlorine or ammonia added. It had a rotten-egg smell to it and I had to plug my nose to drink it, but it was clean. I hauled my stinky water and tired ass back up the hill, collapsed onto my stump and thought how good Dad's leather recliner would feel.

I looked out over the view, pretending this was my own wide-screen TV. Maybe there was only one channel, but shit happened, didn't it? Please let something happen.

A minute later, two ducks came in for a landing on the pond, creating two wakes which eventually joined up into one big V. Thank you, God. And a few minutes after that, a serious number of crows lifted up out of the trees in the valley, creating a cawing black cloud that swirled around the sky before coming up the hill toward me. Wings pounding the air overhead, they momentarily darkened the sky and finally disappeared behind the forest.

Better than the IMAX, I thought.

My stomach growled. What to scrounge for dinner?

I heard the shuffle of leaves in the woods behind me and my instincts went on alert. Bird? Chickadees, I'd discovered, were disproportionately noisy in underbrush.

A twig snapped. Deer or human? Then a hiss and a "What the…" Definitely not a deer.

"Davis, hey."

"Hey." His hair had snagged on a branch and he whipped his head back and forth, whimpering.

"It's a jungle out here," I laughed.

"No shit." He held onto his hair with his free hand – he

was carrying stuff – and pulled, leaving strands of hair hanging in the tree. "Afraid I was lost."

"Some bird's going have a Davis hair nest."

"Feckin' trees."

I had to laugh. "How did you get here?"

"Hitched."

Out of respect for the D.s, I'd asked Davis to come by way of the park and not the road. I didn't want them to think this was going to become some teen party place.

"So this is your new cave, huh? The garden of Gray."

"Check it out." I pointed at the so-called tent behind me.

"Pretty sparse," he said, peering through the net at my bed, a crate for a side table, a hurricane lamp with its half-burned candle, one old pressback chair, a table with hot-plate, dishes and a glass bowl for washing, and some concrete blocks and boards that held my clothes, soap, towel and dry goods box.

"Got to start somewhere. What's in the bag?"

"Mom Two made you some banana bread," he said, handing it over. "No preservatives, organic flour, organic bananas, unpasteurized honey, yada, yada."

"Hey, say thanks from me."

"She also sends Jesus's love," he said in a sticky voice. "She's become 'Jesufied.'" He pumped quotations into the air. "At dinner a couple nights ago, she announced all teary-eyed that she'd found Jesus at her AA meeting. I said I never knew Jesus was a drunk, and Dad gave me a back hander." He pushed aside his hair and showed me a neat little cut dissecting one eyebrow and the yellowing bruise. It looked like it hurt.

"Ow."

"Wedding ring." Davis shrugged. "Anyway, she's starting up a Jesi collection."

"Jesi?" I asked.

"Plural of Jesus," he said with a crooked smile. "She's been putting crucifixes around the house."

"There was one in the kitchen last time I was – "

"Now there's one over their bedroom door and one over the toilet in my bathroom. The way his head droops down, I swear he's trying to check out my self."

I laughed.

"Serious creepage is what it is," he said. "I may have to move in with you."

"Acres of room." I spread my hands, then held the loaf to my nose. It smelled banana good.

"Hey, guess who I ran into in the hall of mediocre learning today?" he said, looking around for a place to sit before he flopped down on the ground.

"Who?"

"That Ciel girl."

I don't know why, exactly, but my stomach did a little jig.

"She gave me a note addressed to you. A crush, maybe?"

"She hates me."

He dug an envelope out of his pocket but didn't hand it to me.

"Hey, did you ever hear this Norris joke," he said, ignoring the fact that I was staring at his hand. "If you have five dollars and Chuck Norris has five dollars…" He slowed down for the punch line. "Chuck Norris has more money." He laughed his messed-up laugh and slapped his knee with Ciel's letter, bending it in half.

"Good one," I said, forcing a laugh.

"But here's another. This is like the best one. Ready?"

"Ready." I forced my eyes off the letter.

"It's a farm joke for you," he said. "Chuck Norris on the farm."

"Go on," I said, impatient.

"Okay, okay. It's about crop circles. You know what those are?"

"I know what they are."

"All right. Ready?"

I just stared at him.

"Crop circles are Chuck Norris's way of telling the world that sometimes corn just needs to…" His voice turned tough. "…lie the fuck down."

As Davis was killing himself laughing, I stood up and snatched the letter from his hand. "Give me that."

"Sometimes corn just needs to lie the fuck down," he repeated, then rolled up off the ground and did a hand-stand on my stump.

The envelope looked like homemade paper. The kind made from recycled old paper matted together with glue and water. I wondered if she'd made it herself. On the front, my name was written in perfect textbook script. I got a little rush picturing her bent over a desk and focusing those X-ray eyes of hers on my little name. On the back of the envelope was a stick figure drawing of a girl flying sideways. She wore a triangle skirt, her arms stuck out to the side, four squiggly lines of hair blowing behind her, a small smile on her round head.

Sky dancer, I thought, liking it. I opened the letter.

Gray, How are you Just wanted to say that I think what you're doing, living off the land and trying not to pollute, is really admirable. I didn't expect it from you. Ciel.

What did she mean she didn't expect it of me? Snooty bitch. Did she think I was some sort of loser making good?

I crumpled up the note and stuffed it in my pocket.

"What did smart girl say?" asked Davis.

"Nothing."

Davis and I hunted in the forest for these edible ferns I'd read about. We didn't find any. Maybe they didn't come out until later in the spring. A jackrabbit bounded across the path and I couldn't help wonder what wild rabbit tasted like. For dinner we ate the Jesus loaf and drank a bottle of organic goat's milk. I'd bought the milk from a guy up the road who, lamely enough, had a goatee.

"Hey, I almost forgot to ask," said Davis. He was about to leave so he could hitch back before dark. "My dad's first wife's sister-in-law — "

"Once removed."

Davis sneered. "Yeah, anyway, she's a journalist and I told her what you're doing and she thinks it's cool and wants to know if she can come interview you for some high-brow mag she works for. Probably bring a photographer." He framed the air with his hands. "Gray Fallon," he said, "Poster Boy for the Generation of Despair."

I laughed, though I liked the idea of having my face in some mag. Imagined Ciel seeing it. I'd have to think of smart-sounding stuff to say. Make her realize she didn't know me from dick.

"Chuck Norris roundhouse kicks the generation of despair with one foot tied behind his back." Davis horked out a laugh.

"Tell her sure. Why the hell not?"

15 Maggie

Saturday morning I biked home for the weekend. Mr. D. had me pruning the orchard all day Friday, and I could feel every fiber of every muscle as I pedaled up the hill out of the valley. At this rate, I was going to be Chuck Norris buff in no time. I imagined running into Natalie at the pool this summer, her checking out my six-pack and begging me to take her back. I pictured Dad being a jerk and me shoving him, his eyes widening with fear at my strength. Oh yeah.

The closer I got to the city, the denser the traffic grew and the dirtier the air. Maggie should not be breathing this shit, I thought, angry at the world all over again.

Ten minutes from home, some major clouds moved in and it started pouring. I was soaked to the skin in minutes. I wondered if my "tent" would keep my bed dry, my floor from turning to mud. My sleeping bag was sure to get nailed. Maybe Mom had a wool blanket I could take back.

Dad wasn't home but Mom was. She was all hyper concerned that I take a hot shower, change into dry clothes. She was cutting crustless sandwiches into triangles for a little party she was throwing for Maggie. Seemed so distracted I'm not sure she realized I'd been away all week. She didn't ask me one question about the farm.

"What kind of party?" I asked before going downstairs to shower.

"A surprise. I just want every day to be memory making."

She looked terrible. Pale and pinch-faced. Her hair was greasy and there was a stain on her shirt the color of urine.

"We're going to silkscreen headbands, play charades, have lunch. High tea, I'm calling it, except there won't be tea but pomegranate juice. Maggie's up to four glasses a day. It's supposed to work wonders. We're having organic cucumber sandwiches on spelt bread, fried tofu with sesame sauce, grapes and macrobiotic carrot cake." She quick-stepped to the oven to check the cake. "The girls should be here in half an hour."

"You know you have a stain…" I pointed at her shirt.

"Oh, I'll have to change." She ran a hand through her hair, adding a streak of macrobiotic mayo to the grease.

I didn't say anything. Hoped she'd find it when she changed her shirt.

"Mag's upstairs?"

"Yes, in bed. Get out of those clothes first. And she's a little tired after last night."

"Last night?"

"Dad took her out to dinner and a movie."

He better not have fed her movie food crap, I thought angrily as I went downstairs to shower.

Man, did that water feel good. It was hard but I cut it

short, refusing to get sucked into a consumer mentality. As I got dressed, I contrasted my near-empty tent to the load of stuff in my sweet: TV, Xbox 360, DVD player, laptop, iPod, hot tub, drawers full of clothes, a closet full of shoes.

I made a vow that I wouldn't touch any of it. All this stuff contributed to the carcinogens of this world – the electronics were run by coal-fired plants, the clothes grown with pesticides, the shoes made from petroleum, the hot tub littered with chlorine.

I made one exception. The computer. But I'd only use it to do research related to Maggie. Well, and to download pics from my camera. My camera didn't count in my mind. It was too much a part of me and I'd taken some cool shots at the farm I wanted to see. Besides, I was making enough sacrifices. Unlike Dad who couldn't even give up his shampoo.

Back upstairs, I heard talking in the living room and quietly angled myself by the wall. Maggie sat on the couch, slouched so that her head rested against its back. The smile plastered on her face looked like effort. Her three closest friends sat huddled on the other side of the coffee table, as if they were afraid to get too close. Mom, still wearing the same stained shirt, hair no cleaner, was arranging paper and pencils on the table.

"Oh, I forgot my color chart," she muttered and hurried off.

There were flowers in a jar on the coffee table, a green ribbon around the jar, an Archie mag, some nail polish. Maggie wore a turtleneck even though she hated them, and long pants with socks, hiding her body and its bumps. I hadn't seen her in a week and her head looked bigger to me. I couldn't figure it out at first, then realized that the rest of her must have shrunk. That she must be losing weight.

The girls started talking about a "super hard" test that Maggie had missed and laughing about some Kyle kid flipping a quarter in the air and catching it whenever the teacher turned his back. Maggie smiled and listened, laughed weakly along.

Making sure Mom wasn't about to walk back in, one of the girls lifted up her hair and showed Maggie a red football-shaped mark on her neck. A hickey. Maggie made a face and one girl laughed behind her hand.

"Hamish," the third girl said, "at a party at Bethany's last night."

Hamish, I recalled, was the name of the boy Maggie had a crush on last year.

"Okay," Mom announced as she came through the dining room, all hyper-bright. "Who wants to design their headband?"

I heated up some tofu cutlets I found in the fridge, along with some brown rice and veggies. After Nacie's lunches, this stuff tasted like cardboard but I ate it anyway. Then I called Davis. Just because I vowed not to play Xbox at my house didn't mean I couldn't play it at his.

By the time I got home, the girls were gone. Mom was in the kitchen pouring rice into a cup. She tossed the empty plastic bag in the garbage.

I went and pulled it out.

"This can be recycled along with other bags."

"Oh, sorry, Gray. Just tuck it under the sink, then."

"And these peelings, Mom. Why aren't they in the compost?" I began picking them out. "And," I continued, picking out a Styrene egg carton, "you should only buy eggs in cardboard unless you're going to drive across town to the depot that takes these."

"Well, the compost outside is full and I haven't gotten around to doing any gardening this year yet and the free-range local are coming in those cartons so I don't – "

"The Daskaloffs have this giant farm and don't generate any garbage." I left out the fact that they burned a lot of stuff in the stove.

"Yes, yes. I'll work on it, Gray," she said, looking up from her cookbook. "I am trying. Now, please, will you take Maggie up her pomegranate juice and eight of these turmeric pills? I'm behind on those banners…"

"Yeah, I was going up anyway. But are you going to buy a second compost bin? Or you know, you can just dump peelings and eggshells and stuff directly on the garden and dig it in." I didn't want to bug her but really…

"Yes, I will. One or the other. Now I'm trying to figure out this recipe."

I knew when I wasn't wanted. Upstairs, I listened at the door in case Maggie was asleep, heard the TV so knocked and pushed open the door.

She was in bed, propped against a wall of pillows. Her desk had been pulled over beside the bed and on it were her three jars of putrefied rice, notebook, laptop, TV remote and a *Young Scientist* magazine.

"Hey, Mag."

"When did you get home?" Her eyes brightened to see me. Made me feel all right. But she didn't lift her head off the pillow, didn't move a muscle, only her eyes. She had taken off her turtleneck, and eraser-sized bumps ran down the right side of her neck. Creeped me out. I couldn't look at her and picked up one of the trolls from her collection and pretended to be interested in its bulbous nose and blue hair.

"Just before the party."

"How's the farm?"

"Major hard work but cool."

"And your tent?"

I laughed. "My tent's all right. A little cold at night. Probably get soaked with this rain."

"You see lots of animals?"

"Lots of deer, though the Daskaloffs' dog scares them off pretty quick. Then there's your mice, raccoons, lots of different birds like hawks and turkey vultures. Bullfrogs at the pond. And bats come out at dusk."

"Cool. Bats keep the mosquitoes away."

"There's still plenty of those." I pulled up my hair and showed her the ring of bites at the back of my neck.

"You know it's only the female mosquitoes that bite you. They need the blood to feed their babies. They can't help themselves."

"Yeah," I said, though I actually didn't know that.

"Seen any skunks?"

"I've smelled skunk but no, haven't seen one."

"I did a report on skunks," she said. "In grade five."

I stifled a yawn, flipped through her science nerd mag.

"They're really friendly. Get along with all sorts of animals like foxes and raccoons, and don't smell unless they activate their scent glands. They give predators a warning first, by raising their tails and stamping their front feet."

She coughed as if her little speech took it out of her. I put down the magazine.

"So you're hanging in there?" I asked and sat in her desk chair, far enough away that I didn't have to notice her tumors.

"I wish Mom would relax. It's like she's trying to kill me with fun."

"Just tell her. I'll tell her."

"She doesn't listen. She's too busy finding some new cure." She glanced at her bright red juice. "Or planning the next fun activity." Maggie sighed. "And Dad's like so mad at Mom. He's been sleeping in the guest room."

"He's a jerk."

Maggie stopped and turned her whole head to look at me. "He's just really scared. It's because of me they're not getting along."

"It's not your fault."

"When I'm gone, I hope they — "

"Don't talk like that!" I said, louder than I meant to. I picked up a jar of rice. "You should throw this moldy crap out already. You've finished your project, haven't you?"

"Just have to write a clean copy of my report." She reached for papers on her desk and started to order them. I could feel another speech coming. I'd try to look interested.

She passed me the papers. On top was a photocopied picture of a water crystal.

"The first picture," she explained, "is of water from a clean glacier lake and the rest are of that same water after it was exposed to different things."

The glacier crystal had a clear space in the center and six protruding points. And each point was intricately detailed. It was the kind of radically complex symmetry that only nature could do.

"Cool," I said to make her feel good, but it really was a neat photo.

"So that's the Before picture," Maggie explained. "And these are the After pictures."

Exposed to classical music, its crystals grew even fancier. Exposed to a heavy metal piece full of swear words made a flat, pockmarked non-crystal of broken concentric circles.

It was a little hard to believe music could have this effect, but the photos were still cool. The next crystal had been exposed to chlorine and looked as though a bomb had knocked out one side of it. The last had been exposed to microwaves and formed no crystals at all.

"Dr. Emoto says it's not that music changes the water. It's a mirror thing," said Maggie. "Water's a mirror of intentions or words. Or something like that." She shrugged and flipped back to the first crystal, the one made from glacier water. "This is the crystal Dr. Emoto says forms again and again in water that's been untouched by human pollution or negative stuff." She traced a finger around it like she was trying to memorize it. "And... this is what's so cool... this same crystal forms when it's exposed to the words gratitude and love. See?" She showed me another identical photo. "Actually, he says it forms with two parts gratitude and one part love. Just like H_2O." She pointed to her laptop. "G_2L I'm calling it in my report," she said proudly. "He says this is the message water's trying to tell us. That feeling two parts gratitude and one part love is the world's true nature."

"What's the difference between love and gratitude?" I asked, wanting her to keep talking and looking, well... so alive.

"Gratitude means letting things be, appreciating things as they are. Love is trying to change things for the better. He says out of love for our family we buy houses and cars and stuff but we forget the gratitude part which cares for the earth, air and — " She stopped suddenly and pressed her arm to her side. "It's time for my medicine."

"Yeah, yeah, okay." I nervously reached for a bottle of pills and handed it to her.

She took two and washed them down with her pomegranate juice.

"You hurt, eh?"

She shrugged. "Not all the time."

Duh, you're on painkillers.

"I think," she said, taking a deep breath, "that, right now, Mom and Dad might have too much love and not enough gratitude."

"I guess," I said, though I didn't really get it.

She fell back on her pillow and had a coughing fit. I looked around feeling useless and ready to get out of here. I was about to call Mom but her coughing finally stopped.

I slapped my hands on my thighs and stood to leave when she stopped me with the words, "I'm not scared to die."

"Well, that's a long way off, so – " I made it as far as the doorway.

"I'm curious, really," she continued, looking out the window, which was now being battered by another downpour. "It feels like I'm going on a trip."

I didn't like this conversation.

"I've been practicing."

"Huh?"

"Yeah, I lie real still, close my eyes so it's all black and just forget about my body. Like it doesn't exist. Then I kind of push into that blackness, to try and sense what's left."

"Like, what's left?" Now *I* was curious.

"Vibrations, I think. Like Dr. Emoto says. Plus whatever frequency my soul, or consciousness, whatever it's called, is vibrating at."

I laughed nervously. "Your soul music."

She nodded. "Yeah. And since I don't know where those vibrations end up, that's the adventure part."

"Well…" I didn't know what to say. Just hoped she wasn't pretending to be chill and that any day she was going to freak out real bad.

"Gray?"

"Yeah?"

"Make sure a window is open when I die," she said. "I think the vibrations will need a way out."

My throat felt thick all of a sudden.

"You got it," I said, trying to sound cool with it. "Mind if I take your picture?" I needed an excuse to leave.

"No."

I went to get my camera, relieved to get out of there.

* * *

I focused on her face, half of which was lit by her lamp, the other half in shadow. She smiled and looked straight at me. Was that a swelling under her eye? I shivered, thinking of that sinus tumor, then took her picture. And a couple more.

"I'll let you rest now," I said.

"I really want some candy."

"What?"

"Dad used to buy me good stuff but Mom found out last week and got all upset."

"Yeah, well, he wasn't doing you any favors."

Maggie sighed. "I just really want some… cinnamon lips."

"They are like full of food coloring and hydrogenated – "

"I don't care," she blurted, sounding more like the old Maggie. "And I want a Blizzard with Smarties and Oreos. Just one. I have money in my jewelry box."

"Maggie, I'm not going to buy you crap food – "

"Please, Gray. Just a Blizzard, that's all. A small one. I won't ask again. I'll pay you," she said. "Please, Gray." She looked so sad. And sick.

"Okay," I said. "But don't tell Dad. Or Mom. Don't tell anybody I did this."

"Okay, I promise. My money's in my – "

"I don't want your money."

I grabbed my jacket off the coat rack and, since it was raining, some goofy plaid golf-tourney cap of Dad's.

I will not look up Blizzard ingredients on the Net. I will not look up Blizzard ingredients on the Net. I will not look up Blizzard ingredients on the Net...

16 Ciel

Wearing Dad's dumb hat, I prayed I wouldn't run into anybody I knew. Dairy Queen was only five blocks away, after all. I walked fast and kept my head down.

As I rounded the corner onto Market Street, I saw Ciel coming out of Maria's deli. Something in me perked right up. Then I remembered her letter and went suddenly spastic over whether or not to turn around or cross the street.

But then she looked up.

"Gray? Is that you?"

"Yeah, hi?" She looked prettier than I remembered. Really pretty, actually. I remembered my hat and yanked it off.

"What are you doing here? I thought you were living out on that farm?"

"Yeah, well, I come home on the weekends."

"Oh, right," she said with a little snicker. "It's just a school-day getaway."

"No. You don't see." I suddenly didn't care how pretty or smart she was. I was tired of her snooty shit. "The only reason I come back each weekend is to see my dying sis-

151

ter." I gave the word dying a little shove and then couldn't stop myself from adding, "Because the doctor says it could be any day now."

Ciel's face turned red, her whip-smart eyes flinching. I thought she might have some cutting comeback but then her voice seemed to catch in her throat.

"I'm… really sorry," she said, shaking her head. "I say stupid things sometimes. I really should go." She dropped her head and ran into the rain.

I watched her go, not quite knowing what had just happened. But hell, I wasn't going to feel bad. Maybe she'd treat me with more respect next time.

I realized I hoped there was a next time.

I opened the door to Dairy Queen, saw Parm and Hughie in line and backed out. Parm was cool but I wasn't in the mood for Hughie.

I walked around the block in the rain, waiting for them to leave.

* * *

I hid the Blizzard in my jacket and snuck it past Mom. Upstairs, I locked Maggie's door and watched the Nature channel with her, some program on polar bears and the melting of their "land mass" due to climate change and how they had to swim miles and miles to find solid ice and were drowning in the process. Really cheerful stuff but Maggie was into it.

"We have to stop polluting so much," she said, spooning her Blizzard into her mouth with its red plastic spoon and disposable cup. "Like why can't they make tailpipes for cars that clean the exhaust? I've read about these scrubbers they put inside factory chimneys to clean up their smoke. Why can't we put scrubbers in tailpipes?"

"I don't know."

She spooned up her Blizzard.

"Tastes like heaven," she groaned.

She didn't seem aware of what she'd said. I took another picture, ice cream dribbling off her lip, a guilty smile, scraggly witch hair. Just another kid pigging out on junk food.

After the show was over and the Blizzard gone, Maggie said she was tired and was going to take a nap before dinner.

"Probably the Blizzard, you know, drained your energy," I said, tucking the empty cup and plastic spoon under my shirt to recycle somehow without Mom noticing.

"It was worth it," she said, smiling.

I went and made a file on my computer named Maggie and downloaded all the pictures I'd taken of her.

It was only me, Mom and Dad for dinner. Maggie hadn't woken up from her nap.

"I've checked on her," Mom said as she placed a beige-colored casserole on the table. "Her breathing's normal and no temperature. Just a nap. It's only a nap."

"What's this?" asked Dad, just sounding curious, really, but I felt Mom bristle.

"Tofu quiche with a buckwheat crust," she said. "And I've made onion rice patties and some beet greens."

"Sounds good," I said, looking hard at Dad.

Though it was Saturday and his day off, Dad had spent the day at the office and had just arrived home as we sat down to eat. He asked how my week went. I answered him in as few words as possible, though I did slip in that some magazine wanted to come out and interview me. He didn't respond.

"That should be interesting," said Mom.

I asked him how his week was and he said, "Fine. Busy." He'd turned into some humorless goon. He and I ate in silence after that, Mom filling the space with not very interesting stories about today's silkscreen disasters. Then she announced that the bank opening was in less than two weeks and she was going to "finish those banners if it kills me."

I said no to carrot tofu pudding and headed over to Davis's. Hoped he had some bud. Getting high sounded awfully good.

His dad and Mom Two were out, though one of his half-brothers and friends were there, drinking beer and watching the game, the smell of hot wings spicing the air.

"You gotta see my girls," Davis said, pulling me into his room. He opened the cabinet and I couldn't even see the peat pots for all the greenery. They were bushy, a foot tall and one mass of fluttering green leaves. The hole in the back had been made bigger and a little fan was blowing on them.

"I need a place to plant them real fast or they're toast."

"I'd say. What's the fan for?"

"To strengthen the stalks so once they're outside the wind won't destroy them. I read about it online."

"Makes sense."

"Had to Chuck Norris two of them."

"Why?"

"Turned out to be male. The females get these pre-flowers, see? The males get little balls and a piston."

"No way."

"So, Gray?"

"Yeah?"

"What about where you're staying?"

"What about it?"

"For my girls. On that giant property, the owners wouldn't even notice a few more green things along one edge of – "

"Are you kidding?"

"Well, then what about in the woods behind your tent? That's not their property, it's parkland. When I came to see you there was this nice little clearing not – "

"That would be pretty sketchy."

"They'd never know. And you wouldn't have to do anything. Maybe throw some water on them if it like hasn't rained for a while. And I'll give you half. We could sell it to those guys out there in the living room in like a minute. You and I'd make some serious cash."

"Now we're dealing?"

"No. Just to my brothers and their friends. That's not dealing. That's sharing. We share our bud and they share their money."

I was pretty strapped for cash. And I wasn't about to ask Dad for any money.

"Being Mr. Clean and all, I thought you'd appreciate

some organic weed." Davis smiled hopefully. "We'll know what we're smoking, at least. And we won't like ever have to go without."

That was a nice thought.

"You got any tonight?" I asked.

"Nope. Nada."

Shit. I really felt like getting ripped.

"So, all I'd have to do is water them once in a while?"

"That's it, I swear." Davis perked up. "I'll plant them, come and feed them their hula food every week. Sing to them. You only have to water them. And that's only if there's no rain. If it rains, you do nothing, just reap the rewards." He looked at me all eager.

"Okay, but only if you get me wrecked tonight."

"Yes." Davis pumped his fist.

"Organic, eh? We should charge extra for that."

"Double," said Davis, leaning over his plants. "You're going to have a new home, girls. Pack your buds, we're hitting the road."

Davis bought a sliver of a joint off one of the guys in the living room. We got ripped and did some gaming, chowing down on the half a pepperoni pizza and garlic dip Davis's brother threw our way. I wasn't going to eat any but Mom's macro dinner wasn't very filling, and being stoned I was messed up hungry.

When I got home that night, the house was dark. I popped on my laptop to check my messages, forgetting I'd vowed not to. Also forgetting that nobody was sending me messages these days.

But tonight there was something. From Ciel.

hi. just wanted to apologize for today. I don't mean to come off like a jerk, it's just some weird defense thing. Being new here and all, I'm not really myself. Anyway, I'm so sorry about Maggie and what I said. Friends I hope. Ciel

I was about to write back to say no problem. Tell her that I did stupid things all the time.

But then I thought no. I'd play it cool for a change. Let her hang a little.

17 Skunkweed

Davis grabbed a shovel and put on his backpack, which held a bag of organic compost/peat moss, a Baggie full of lime to sweeten the soil, and his girls. I grabbed my water jug and camera. I'd started using the D.s' electricity to recharge my camera, too. Hoped they didn't mind. Was still waiting to hear from that solar company.

We hiked up into the woods. I had just finished work, digging and more digging around the base of the plum and cherry trees. Something to do with root rot. I think I pulled a groin muscle.

"I'm not digging the holes," I told Davis.

"That's fine. Leave it to me. Hey, my dad has a bet going with my brother Sam over how long you'll last out here."

"What's the bet?"

"My dad says a month. Sam's giving you till the end of June."

"How much on the table?"

"Fifty."

"Ask if they'll give me the money if I last past June."

"Yeah, right."

"I might just live out here forever." My tent had survived the weekend's rain no problem. My sleeping bag was wet and I had to hang it out in the sun, but the trees kept the rest pretty dry.

"Forever's a long feckin' time. What, are they going to adopt you?"

While Davis hunted for a hidden clearing to plant his girls, I hunted mushrooms for dinner. Puffballs, that is, those stemless ball-shaped things that shot out brown smoke when you stepped on them. You had to pick puffballs before the spores developed. Fried up in olive oil with a little garlic and salt, they were delicious. And if I came across some stinging nettle I'd throw those in with it.

Nothing, I'd decided, tasted better than fresh-picked food. Especially if it was wild. You could taste wildness. It tasted like pulsing color in your mouth. Like your mouth was stoned or something.

I found nearly half a dozen puffballs but no nettle, and Davis found his clearing. It was dangerously close to the D.s' property, only ten yards behind my tent. But then I wouldn't have to haul water very far, I thought, and went ahead and helped him remove some of the ferns and dead leaves.

I watched as he dug and prepared four holes.

"Okay, girls," said Davis as he wiped the dirt from his hands and stood back admiring his work. "I'd like something strong enough to make me see God. Or Chuck Norris. I want to see Chuck Norris. No, I want to *be* Chuck Norris."

Then, because the sun was now reflecting off these gray storm clouds that had rolled in over the valley and the light was all silvery, I took some pictures.

I made Davis climb up an oak and hide among the leaves, showing only part of an arm and one foot. Then had him show only his nose and chin. Then an ear and one hand. We did similar shots under this ground cover of spiny yellow flowers, like sea anenomes, and then again in the rye grass field.

"Hey, what do you think of Ciel?" I asked as I helped him up off the ground.

He studied me for a second. "I think she's all right. A lot higher up the food chain than your last one. In fact, you might be shooting a little high there, Gray."

"Just because she gets As in school doesn't mean she's smarter than me."

"Now that was a dumb thing to say."

"Forget it."

"I'll ask her at school tomorrow if she wants to screw you."

"Go ahead and I'll rip your girls out by their tender little roots."

"Ooh. I think you like her."

I shoved him.

"Ciel and Gray," he said, trotting backwards and away from me. "Her name means sky, right? So together you'd be Gray Sky. Sounds like one cheerful couple."

Wanting to try out my new muscle, I ran at him and wrestled him to the ground. But he was laughing so hard, it was all too easy.

Davis didn't stay for dinner, but I collected four eggs from a nest I'd seen earlier behind the compost, a hothouse tomato, fresh basil and parsley.

Back at my tent, I set a pot of water to boil for noodles. The bullfrogs had begun their evening croakfest down at the pond. Mincing garlic, I started to count their croaks. By the time the pasta was ready, I was up to two hundred and six. Nacie told me those frogs were an alien species that were taking over and killing off smaller frogs. And that they were the type of frog the French used to make their famous frog legs, which are supposed to taste just like chicken. She said I was more than welcome to catch them and cook them up. Yeah, right.

After the sun went down, I hit the outhouse, came back and watched the bats flit around in their silent bat way catching their dinner. The mosquitoes were bad and a few wouldn't leave me alone. Inside my tent, I kept swatting at them until I decided it was easier to let them suck on me already and go feed their babies. My bag, still damp on one side, was cold in the night air.

I masturbated to get to sleep. Started out picturing Natalie and her excellent breasts but she suddenly turned into a slender figure with pale brown hair, coppery eyes, palm-sized breasts…

Gray Sky was my last thought before the world disappeared.

*   *   *

In the middle of the night, I woke not knowing where I was. It took a panicky minute to remember. There was no moon or stars so it was seriously black. If I closed my eyes there was more light.

Sometimes it was the cold that woke me or a sound, but tonight I think it was the silence. Nothing was louder than black silence.

Because there was dick-nada to hear, I moved my leg just to prove I wasn't some disembodied thought floating in space.

Just as I turned over to go back to sleep, I did hear something – a rattle, then a crunching in the underbrush. Bears were the first thing that came to mind. Psychopaths a close second. My heart was playing my eardrums like bongos.

Nobody would hear me if I screamed. The neighbors were too far away, the D.s' place was a hundred yards down the hill.

More crunching and rattling, louder and therefore coming closer. My breathing was as small as I could make it without passing out. The dark could fool a person but not an animal. A bear would smell me, not to mention the dirty frying pan I'd left on the table. Could bears see in the dark?

When the noise was right outside my tent, I imagined a man on the other side of the net wall standing beside my bed. He could lift that net, reach out and…

Real quietly I reached for my hand-crank flashlight, praying the light still had juice in it.

I pointed it at the sound, muscles primed to bolt, and pressed it on.

Nothing. Just netting and blackness beyond. Then something was moving again on the left, close to the ground. I swung the light over.

Big as a raccoon, this skunk stood on its hind legs staring into the beam. Its pointy nose sniffed the air and my lungs collapsed in relief. Then three baby skunks appeared from behind it and, copying their mother, tried to stand up, too.

Maggie would be too excited to see this, I thought. One little runt tried to use his brothers' backs as support and ending up knocking them all over like fluffy black bowling pins.

I grabbed my camera and turned it on. When the flash popped, they all froze, the mother especially, her tail now sticking up in the air.

Shit. Afraid my house might never smell the same again, I clicked off my flashlight and lay back down.

Don't spray my tent, please, please, please.

Hoped I got a decent picture for Maggie.

18   Poster Boy

The magazine lady showed up the next day.

Poured into her tight black clothes, her black hair was cut like Cleopatra, exposing a scary-white forehead. She wore pointy cowboy boots and smoked clove cigarettes. She looked depressed. Her name was Harry, for Harriet. Her mirrored sunglasses never came off and I could see two of me in their reflection as I answered her questions.

It was pretty distracting. Stoner stuff.

I told her I refused to go back to school because the walls were filled with asbestos and they sold cancer foods in their vending machines. (I had practiced things I could say.) I listed the many ways, from toothpaste to car exhaust, soap to drywall, that we were poisoning ourselves in the name of progress. And pointed out that people were getting rich making toxic stuff that was killing people, fish and whatever else. The government not doing dick about it.

I talked a lot about Maggie, made it sound like she could die any second and even got choked up a little. I was determined, I told her, to show people that we could live without polluting.

I was pretty pumped watching her scribble on her pad of paper quoting me. Thought I sounded damn smart, too. Dad, I bet, was going to feel different after seeing this article. I mean, somebody thought what I was doing was important enough to write about, didn't they?

"What would you recommend to people? Product wise."

"Stay away from anything with ingredients you can't pronounce."

Harry sneered, which I think was her way of smiling, then asked if they knew specifically what caused Maggie's cancer.

"I'm still trying to sort that out. I mean, it's not like her friends at school have it or any of the neighbor kids. They're all exposed to the same crap."

Though Harry looked just as depressed as when she arrived, she said she was really happy with the interview. And that she would send me two free copies of the magazine when it came out.

I had to ask her why she smoked when it was so carcinogenic.

"I hate myself," she answered flatly, took a last puff and dropped the butt to grind under her boot.

Oddly enough, the local rag came around the next day, even took my picture. And then a couple of days later, while I was cleaning the mold off the hothouse windows, some environmental magazine called *E* showed up. The guy drove an electric scooter and wore "fiber-friendly" clothing, as he called it. He was into "waking people up to their toxic lives," and he made me feel like some sort of hero. When I asked how he'd heard about me, he said a friend of his at Solar Enterprises had passed on my story.

"Really? Does that mean they might give me some free panels and stuff?"

"I can't say for sure, but my friend's pushing for you."

"Cool."

He left me a couple of their mags, then sadly got nailed by Clarence (front of the knee) as he was putting on his helmet. It made him stumble and nearly fall over his scooter.

After the guy left, I went back to cleaning the greenhouse windows. I pictured the article being posted on the school bulletin board. Imagined Ciel seeing it.

* * *

Before I biked home on Saturday, I filled my two jugs with water, nabbed a bucket of compost and went to feed Davis's girls.

Judging by how green and bushy they were, they were loving their new forest home. Anything had to be better than Davis's desk cabinet. I swear they were a lot bigger already but maybe that was because they had room to spread out. I tossed some compost around their stalks and gave them a good drenching.

First thing I did when I got home was to check MSN. I'd decided on the bike home that it was okay to use my computer to not only do research but to check my mail. Because what if some journalist was trying to track me down?

I was kind of hoping there'd be something from Ciel but there wasn't.

* * *

My weekend was spent babysitting Maggie because Mom was off doing a weekend conference called "Cancer and the Food We Eat" and Dad was in Chicago giving a paper. So it was just Maggie and me. I showed her my shot of the skunks which had come out well.

Then, though I'd already heard most of it, I let her read her finished science fair report to me. Monday was the start of the fair. Maggie was too tired to go herself so Mom had worked it out that she would take the project over and Maggie's science teacher would present it to the judges.

That night I called Davis and begged him to come over. To give babysitting more dimension, he arrived with some weed and we blazed on the back porch. Back inside, we played cards with Maggie for awhile and then watched a movie together. Mom had bought some organic "treats" to help satisfy Maggie's junk-food cravings. We ate organic popcorn with flax oil instead of butter and gummi bears made from fruit juice and seaweed. Being stoned, anything tasted good. Davis and I both drank pomegranate juice with Maggie. That actually tasted really good.

I wasn't that interested in the movie and kept stealing glances at Maggie.

I didn't think it was my stoned imagination. I truly think she was looking stronger. And the tumors didn't seem as noticeable. Maybe the steps Mom and I had taken were finally making a difference. She was getting better slowly but surely.

Doctors didn't know everything after all. Dad would have to choke on his words when Maggie recovered. I pictured him bowing at my feet.

After the movie, I took a bunch of pictures of Maggie and Davis making goofy faces together. Davis got Maggie to laugh a lot. Laughing led her to have a coughing fit but I didn't worry about it because I remembered hearing somewhere that laughing was healing. Besides, how sick could she be if she could still laugh?

It hit me how much stronger I felt since living and working on the farm. If Maggie could live there, she'd get better even faster.

19 Boo Yeah

Pushing a hand tiller up the potato field, I hit another rock. Thinking of how I owned Dad over the weekend, I heaved that rock up the hill into the woods.

Two of those articles on me had come out and on the weekend I'd arrived home to a pile of letters supporting my cause and asking my advice. Mom was hyper-proud, and even Dad had to admit I was "making a difference for some people."

I'd even gotten a letter from Ciel, sort of, but really it was from the E-Club at school. They'd written the school board demanding that asbestos be removed from the walls and healthier stuff be put into the vending machines. They sent me a copy of the letter, Ciel's name one of eight who'd signed at the bottom. It had to be her who brought me up to the club. Who else?

Though it had taken up most of my weekend, I answered each letter. Some, like me, had family or friends fighting cancer. Some had cancer themselves. One woman thanked me for trying to "clean up this country's cancer minefield." That was a pretty dice image and I thought I'd use it in my next interview.

My shovel hit another rock. I pried it up, tossed it on the pile.

Maggie had won a blue ribbon for her science project. We had a celebration dinner and Mom gave in to Dad and cooked Maggie's favorite meal, though the ribs were from un-medicated cows and the potatoes and peas organic.

I finished tilling the last row and could tell by where the sun hung in the sky that it was near quitting time. I was covered in sweat. I needed a shower. Which meant I had to decide whether to stand under a freezing-cold hose or jump in the pond. Because I used non-toxic soaps, the D.s didn't mind me washing in their pond, which had warmed up with the weather.

I was digging out my shampoo when I heard Litze's throaty growl down by the barn. Some girl in sunglasses was pointing at the dog and backing up. She was saying something to Mr. D. that I couldn't hear.

I had a crazy thought that it was Ciel. That she'd come to apologize.

I squinted to see better. Brown hair, thin. Litze came wagging over to her, his massive head bowed for a pat. She didn't pat him. Then Mr. D. said something and pointed in my direction.

My stomach seemed to jump up and bang into my throat. God, I looked like shit and smelled even worse. I'd taken off my shirt but grabbed it again. It stank worse than me. Did I even have any clean shirts? I had purposely stopped taking laundry home on the weekends to prove I didn't need modern conveniences. Had been meaning to hand-wash stuff in the outdoor sink and hang it out but...

Another dog growl and a guy – with two heads? – was coming up the path. No, a black box was perched on his shoulder. A camera?

I could see now it wasn't Ciel. The woman and camera guy continued up the path and I saw Clarence sneak out from behind the workshop. The woman screamed as he nailed the back of her knee. Ouch. He hopped in the air, then toddled off. The woman rubbed her leg and said something to the camera head.

I settled back on my stump to watch them pick their way up the dirt path.

The woman finally saw me.

"Graydon? Graydon Fallon?" she called out before stumbling on a rock. The camera which had been aimed at her now panned up to me.

Was he actually filming? I nodded and raised my hand.

Definitely not Ciel, this woman was thirty-something and, as she shoved her sunglasses to the top of her head, heavily made-up. She smelled of perfume. What I thought was a black brooch of some kind on her blouse was actually a microphone.

I was either going to be on television or in some movie.

I combed a hand through my sweat-slick hair.

"So nice to finally meet you." Her voice was loud. She extended her hand. A monarch butterfly floated up and landed on her left hip. She didn't even notice.

"I am so impressed with what you're trying to do,

young man. My name's Cynthia and this is Greg. We're from the nightly news." Greg peeked his very bald head out from behind the camera just long enough to lean forward and shake my hand. Cynthia's handshake was twice as firm as Greg's.

"So I guess you're a Swiss Family Robinson fan?" she said and, not waiting for an answer (which would have been no), walked right past me to peer into my net house.

"Is that thing on?" I asked, pointing at the camera. She didn't answer, nor did Greg. I was wondering if he could talk at all.

"Uh, I was just going to – " I began and Cynthia whipped around and thrust a large black phallus-shaped microphone in my face. "Uh, wash up a bit, put on a clean shirt." Relatively clean, I hoped.

"And where do you do your washing up?" she asked.

"Well, either under the hose or in the pond."

"Oh, will you do the pond for us? That would be just great."

"Yeah, sure."

"Do you bring soap? Shampoo?"

"Uh, I'll use this stuff for both – " I held up my bottle.

"You don't make your own soap?"

"No."

"Oh." She looked disappointed.

I went into my tent and grabbed a towel. I needed to put on my bathing suit but since a TV camera was right outside my see-through house, this meant going down to the outhouse.

"I'm just going to go down to the outhouse and – "

"There's an outhouse?"

They followed me to the outhouse, Cynthia describing everything she saw for the camera. Then they followed me down to the pond. She had me doing a kind of James-Bond-emerging-from-the-water thing several times in a row. They filmed me toweling off and hanging stuff on my laundry line.

When I said I needed to go back to the outhouse to get dressed, she asked if I'd do it in the tent instead.

"We'll turn our backs until you've got your boxers on. The light through the netting will make for a nice shot, wouldn't you say, Greg?"

Greg's camera nodded.

Once I was dressed, she had me sit on my stump and then asked what products I'd recommend people using. I didn't want to repeat what I'd already said in other interviews so I said, "Generally you could think about it this way. Our skin is our biggest and most porous organ. So if you wouldn't put it in your mouth, don't put it on your skin. Because it's no different. So unless you'd roll your scented antiperspirant on your tongue, don't roll it under your arms."

She gave me a big nod and a smile.

I let them film me collecting eggs and picking lettuce greens for dinner. "The yolk of the Daskaloffs' eggs is a deep orange color, not that pale yellow you get from factory chickens. And they taste totally better."

I picked some strawberries, which I offered to them

with some homemade dandelion tea. I topped up our tea cups with a dandelion flower for effect. Cynthia liked that, as I figured she would, her camera man zooming in on her cup.

She asked her questions and I did my best to answer them. When she asked my philosophy on life, I thought of Maggie's science project. I said that I thought people needed to appreciate life more and quit trying to improve it all the time. That nature couldn't be improved on. I told her about this Japanese scientist's (I couldn't remember his name) experiments with water crystals and the G_2L equation. I was going to give Maggie the credit but Cynthia looked so impressed that I didn't bother. Didn't think Maggie would mind.

"I guess you'd call yourself a pretty clean liver?"

"Well, I'm underage so can't drink. I don't drive. I stay away from processed food. And I don't smoke."

She raised her thinly plucked eyebrows, held a pretend joint to her lips.

"No, not that, either," I said. Was she trying to get me arrested or something?

"He doesn't smoke, do drugs, eat junk food, drink or pollute the planet," she said.

"Don't make me out to be some perfect guy," I said, not wanting to come off as some kind of suck.

"Perfection is what the people want," she said with a sideways smile. "I mean, perfection is also what you want, right?"

"Well, you have to admit it's criminal what we're doing

to ourselves. The modern world's a cancer minefield."

She didn't appreciate that one as much as I thought she would.

"How long do you think you'll keep this up?"

"It's a lifestyle change, so I guess forever."

"You can't live in this tent forever, Gray," she said. "Winter's not going to go away."

"No, I'll need more of a shelter at some point." I recalled reading something about a bale house in that *E* magazine the guy left me. "I'm considering building a bale house."

I had to sign a release form, found out the piece would air Saturday night as part of the six o'clock news. I'd be home and able to watch it with Maggie, Mom and Dad. Maybe I'd send out a message telling my friends about it. No, that would seem like bragging. I'd get Davis to do it.

After Cynthia and Greg left, I remembered I hadn't watered Davis's girls for awhile and went to fill my jugs. Davis had left me some African violet plant food to "spike their drink."

The girls were thriving. Bushy and green, leaves all perky. On the biggest plant, which Davis had named Ruth, I noticed a sizeable bud.

Yes. Grow, girls, grow. If I was going to stay here and build some sort of winterized place, I'd need some serious cash. And this would be the easiest cash I'd ever made.

That night I dreamed some movie company came and offered me millions to make a movie of my life. The only stipulation was that I let them cut my hair.

I said sure.

* * *

The next day I was helping Mr. D. haul compost to spread on the growing fields. I had worked damn hard the past weeks and Mr. D. had become a lot friendlier. The lunch bell started clanging and he and I both looked up at the sky and then at each other. Litze started barking excitedly.

"It can't be ten-thirty," grumbled Mr. D.

"Yeah."

"Guess she wants us to come down though."

"Guess so."

There was a large white truck in the drive. Earth Friendly Inc. was painted on its side in blue and green letters. Two men in white jumpsuits, a green-and-blue planet earth logo on their pockets, stood watching us approach. One tall thin guy was smiling real big, his eyes just slits. He looked majorly blazed. Nacie was there, too, smiling away.

The more compact guy walked up to me. He seemed to be in charge of things.

"You Gray Fallon?"

"Yeah."

"It's a good thing you're doing, kid. And that's why we're here to deliver to you, at no cost or catch, a complimentary Sunlight Dome Shelter."

"A what?"

"It's a kind of house," said Nacie. "A donation to the cause."

"But how – "

"We're a sister company of Solar Industries," said the man. "Your solar-powered generator will be delivered tomorrow." He raised an eyebrow. "You could say it's your lucky day. Your lucky week."

No shit.

"Where do you want it?" asked the guy with the stoner grin. He had a ponytail that fell to his waist.

"It's not my property," I said, turning to Mr. D., who looked real concerned.

"Are we going to be some sort of billboard?" he asked. "And are you, Gray, expected to be a salesperson for this dome thing?"

"The way the company sees it," said the boss guy, "is that it's exposure for the dome. You don't have to allow anyone on your property to view it but we are instructed to make it visible from the road. Hey," the guy shrugged, "basically Earth Friendly likes what this kid stands for and wants to help out."

"It would be nice to be a little warmer at night," I said. "Not to mention dryer. Then there's the mosquitoes..." I scratched at my neck for effect. Please, I prayed, don't turn them away.

"This is what you're after, then," grinned ponytail guy. "About the nicest outdoor living you could ask for."

"The dome makes use of passive solar heat," continued the boss. "There's a solar-powered fan for air circulation. Has what we call an earthen floor made of sand, clay, straw and water. This retains heat under your feet. Screens on all the windows will keep out pests. You even got a sink and built-in water purification system. Because you, my friend, are getting the new improved model."

"Amazing," was all I could say. "But, uh… it's not up to me." I looked wide-eyed at Nacie, pleading without pleading. The place sounded incredible. Had to cost a wad.

"I think maybe it could go up on the hill beside your tent?" she suggested, looking amused. "It will look as if we're starting our own colony."

I had to keep myself from whooping.

"Great spot," said the compact guy. "There'll be enough sun for your fan and generator, and the dome will be visible from the road."

"What do you think, Milan?" asked Nacie.

Mr. D. was still frowning. He was about to speak when Nacie turned to the delivery men. "If we don't like it, can we send it back?"

"Sure thing. Just have to call the company." He dug a card out of his pocket. "We'll come dismantle it and take it away."

"So I don't see that we have anything to lose, Milan?"

Mr. D. sighed and gestured up the drive. "All right. Go ahead."

I let out my breath and smiled gratefully at Nacie. "Thanks, thanks so much. This is great."

"Never a dull moment with you here, Gray," she said. "Now, I have to get back to my strawberry jam."

"Come, Gray," said Mr. D., still frowning. "Let's get back to work."

20 On a Roll

"I looked it up on line and the cost is twelve grand." Dad's eyebrows rose at the number and I felt a rush of pride. "You got to come see it. It's amazing."

I'd just finished describing my new house to Mom, Dad and Maggie. We were at the dinner table having dessert: ginger cake with tofu whipped cream. The cake was bitter, the tofu whipped cream a weird thought with a gross texture. I tried to eat it for Maggie's sake but just couldn't.

"There's even a cistern that collects rainwater and kills bacteria with ultraviolet light."

"Hey, in his book, Dr. Emoto says if you use ultraviolet light instead of chlorine – " Maggie coughed a tight, painful-sounding cough, " – it still makes perfect ice crystals."

"Cool. Mag, you should really come out. Breathe the clean country air. You could stay with me now that I have my own place."

"Your own place, huh?" repeated Dad, not meeting my eye.

Yeah, Dad, I wanted to say, only sixteen and I had my own place, was making my own way without your help.

I looked at Mom. "I bet she wouldn't even need the oxygen tank."

Maggie had been having trouble breathing lately and the doctor had prescribed oxygen to make her more comfortable. So up in her room was this noisy machine attached to a long plastic tube that she hooked into her nose. It made me all the more convinced she needed to get out of this house.

"I'm not sure about that, Gray," said Mom.

"I have my own electricity, so she could bring her computer." Maggie wasn't going to school any more but Mom had set up a home-schooling program for her via computer. "And we could bring the tank, though like I said, I doubt she'll need it. You'd be surprised," I said, looking at Dad, "at the air-quality difference out there versus in town here."

"I want to see where Gray lives," said Maggie. She took a deep breath, chest heaving. "We could go look, anyway…" She started to cough.

"Let's get you over this coughing first," said Mom, clearing her own throat. "And, well, I have some news too. I wanted to tell everyone that… I lost that banner commission. Easy come, easy go."

"You've been too busy taking care of –"

"It's not your fault, Maggie," cut in Dad. "Your mom could have found time if she'd wanted to."

Mom glanced down at her hands. "Of course it's not your fault, sweetheart. It was just not that important. You're what's important to me, not some stupid old bank. I'll finish them one day and sell them to another stupid old bank." She laughed, but it didn't sound very cheery.

My parents were too depressing.

"So, Mag, you should come have a sleepover. I'll cook up some farm fresh eggs for you. Spinach is happening, some wild scallions, fresh herbs. I got some goat cheese from this guy down the road. I'll make you the best omelet you've ever tasted. Nacie gave me a great recipe for stinging nettle soup. And she makes excellent oatmeal bread, and brownies you'd kill for."

"I thought I wasn't allowed to eat brownies." Maggie looked at me accusingly. She coughed, took another big breath, then another.

Man, it looked like it hurt her to breathe. She really had to get out of this house.

"Well, Nacie doesn't use any junky ingredients, so it's probably almost macro. I mean, you should see these people. They're both in their sixties and work like twelve-hour days. Heavy work, too."

Mom took another bite of the cake no one else had touched after the first gagging taste.

"Some day this week you'll have to bring her out, Mom."

"I'm just not sure – "

"She can rest there as easy as here. And Mag, my dome has these picture windows and from my bed you can see hawks circling overhead for their lunch, watch the duck action down at the pond. I saw a nest in the cattails so I bet there'll be ducklings soon. And when Litze's inside, deer will come right up to the dome."

Maggie's tired eyes lit up. "Maybe we'll see that skunk again."

"Maybe."

"I really want to go, Mom," she coughed.

"Okay, okay. I'd like to see the dome, too. But I don't know if you should stay out there."

"It would be a lot better than sleeping here," I said and coughed myself just to prove it.

Dad, the spermbag, made a scoffing sound.

"Hey, what time is it?"

"Five to six," said Dad.

"*Nightly News* in five minutes, starring…" I framed my face with my hands.

"We can take our dessert into the living room," said Mom.

I caught Maggie's eye as we picked up our cake plates.

"Brownies," I mouthed.

She licked her lips.

Mine was announced as one of tonight's top stories, boo yeah, though the announcer didn't say when it was coming on. So we sat through some stock market scandal – this English guy losing 8 billion dollars for a London bank – then an update on the war in Iraq before they went to commercial.

"I bet you're next," said Maggie. Every time she spoke she had to take a couple of loud breaths, as if to make up the oxygen.

"Nobody's eating their cake," said Mom.

"I'm pretty full," I said.

"Me, too," said Maggie, catching my eye again.

"Julia, your kids are just being polite. This cake is completely inedible," said Dad.

Mom's spine straightened.

"Well, you could use some of that politeness," she said and noisily collected the plates off the coffee table before disappearing into the kitchen. Then came the sound of things crashing into the sink.

"Nice one, Dad," I said.

Dad pushed back his chair, stood up and left.

"Man, I can't believe you put up with this crap," I said to Maggie. "No wonder you're sick."

Maggie was holding her chest, which was heaving with each breath. Her eyes were half closed, like she might pass out.

"Mom," I called and the panic in my voice brought her back in a flash.

"Upstairs," she said to Maggie, easing her off the couch. "We need to get you hooked up. Come on." Maggie obeyed and they were gone just as I saw Cynthia's face fill the screen. "Welcome to Happy Valley Farm."

Great, I thought, looking around the empty room. I watched the segment alone. Came across even better than I'd thought. I didn't look half bad on camera, either.

I only hoped that Davis had got the word out and that kids from school were watching it. Namely Ciel. Because not only did I sound damn intelligent, my pecs looked all right coming out of the water.

* * *

I was downstairs answering a couple letters that had come that week. There would be a lot more after the TV segment.

Then out of nowhere, it hit me. Why hadn't I thought of it before? What was Maggie exposed to that other kids weren't?

I was typing Silkscreen, Carcinogens, when the phone rang.

"Hello?"

"Hi, Gray. It's Ciel."

"Hey," I said, all excited to hear her voice, then quickly got control of myself. "How's it going?" I said, keeping it cool.

"I saw you on the news tonight."

Make her beg for it, I thought. I didn't respond.

"It was a really great interview."

"Thanks."

"I hope you got the letter from the E-Club."

"Yeah. Got it."

"The head of the school board wrote us back and said they'd look into it."

"It's about time."

"I hope, uh, Maggie's improving."

"Not exactly."

"God, I'm sorry."

"Not your fault. Though maybe it is. All our faults for living like we do and buying the stuff we buy."

"Yeah. You're right."

Yeah, I'm right. Get used to it, I thought.

There was one of those uncomfortable gaps and I let her squirm.

"Well, I just wanted to say it was impressive, your interview."

"Okay, well, thanks for calling."

"Okay, bye."

I hung up. Yeah, she wants me, I thought, swiveling a 360 in my chair.

I looked up at the screen. Benzene is a common chemical found in silkscreen wash-ups.

Bingo.

That had to be it. It was something other kids weren't exposed to, and Mom got into silkscreen about a year or so before Maggie was born. Probably had concentrations of it in her blood when pregnant, so Maggie could have been exposed "in utero" like that doctor said. Hell, Mom used to work in the basement so there was probably benzene in the air, too. And Maggie was always making stuff…

It made perfect scientific sense. And who had figured it out? Not you, Dad.

I was about to bound upstairs when I stopped. This was going make Mom feel guilty as crap. But did I have any choice? No. She had to be told in order to stop exposing Maggie. Couldn't be good for her, either. I had to tell her right away. I mean, Maggie could finally start to get better. That was the important thing.

Mom was in the kitchen, slumped over some cookbook. She didn't hear me walk in and startled when I pulled out the seat beside her.

"Oh, you scared me," she said with a little cry of a laugh. "Sorry to have missed your spot on the news. It's just crazy around here." She smiled lamely. "We caught the very end on Maggie's TV. Oh, I should have taped it." She pressed a hand to her forehead. "Oh, why didn't I tape it? That was just − "

"Yeah, no worries," I said, and then decided just to say it, casual like. "So I found out that there's benzene in silkscreen wash-ups. So Maggie shouldn't do any more of that. And maybe you, too. Unless there's some substitute you can use…"

Mom was no longer listening. Her mouth was open, and she'd gone all glassy eyed.

"It's my fault," she said in a quiet voice.

"No, no, you can't think like that. It's just another thing we should probably avoid − "

"That's why you're okay. But Maggie…" Her voice was all weird and soft.

She stood up, went over to open the deck door and walked outside.

"Where are you going?" She just kept crossing the lawn.

I guess she wasn't wasting any time and wanted to get rid of it right now.

"Need any help?" I called out as she fished down the studio key from the door ledge and opened the eggplant-colored door. She didn't answer, just went in and shut the door behind her.

The light went on and then I heard a crash.

I went outside to the deck. Through one of the windows, I saw my mother hurl a bolt of material across the room. I heard a scream and there was another crash.

Holy shit. I ran into the living room where Dad was just sitting in front of the hockey game.

"Dad. Quick. Mom's in her studio…"

"And…"

"Hurry," I practically yelled, and he gave me a stern look. "She's in trouble."

I went ahead of him onto the deck. The sound of insane screaming and things being thrown filled the yard. Neighbors' porch lights were coming on, heads popping out of back doors. Dad ran across the lawn and tried to open the door.

It was locked. The key was inside with her. He banged on the door.

"Julia. Let me in." Something hurled against the window beside the door. A crack like a bolt of lightning ran the length of the window.

I was glad Maggie's room was at the front of the house and sure hoped she couldn't hear anything.

"I need the spare key," Dad yelled at me as he rattled the doorknob. "On top of the fridge. Get it. Now!"

After Dad unlocked the door, I watched as he tried to wrestle Mom into his arms. She fought him like a crazy person. It freaked me out to see her like this.

The studio was messed. Paint dripped over everything, tables were overturned. The half dozen banners she had managed to finish for the bank, which hung on the walls around the room, were now splashed with ink.

Dad was holding her now, hushing her. Her struggling morphed into whimpering, her head lolling back on her neck. Something wet and dark plastered her hair to the right side of her head.

Paint? Blood?

"It's my fault," she said through her tears. "I did it. It's all my fault."

"Julia, no, it's nobody fault," Dad said, sounding almost angry with her. "What in God's name makes you think that?"

21 Owned

Dad's friend and coworker, a happy science nerd named Brad, drove Maggie out to the farm. While Brad carried her oxygen machine and backpack, I helped Maggie get from the car into the dome.

Mom had flown east for some "R and R," as Dad put it. She was going to spend a couple of weeks with Grammy and Aunt Judy, who would "take care of her, make sure she did nothing but rest." Grammy had been a psychiatric nurse before she retired.

I never told Dad what I'd told Mom about the benzene in the wash-ups. As if I didn't feel terrible enough.

How could I have known it was going to push her over the edge? I couldn't not tell her. And it wasn't her fault. It was the government's fault for allowing the stuff to be sold in the first place. In fact, this week I was going to write a letter to the company that made the wash-ups and another to the government body in charge of testing it.

Dad was taking time off from work to stay home with Maggie, but first he had some big grant application to finish up. So I was getting my wish. Maggie was going to be my guest for the next three nights.

"You want to sit down?" I asked her. I'd borrowed a second chair from Nacie so now had two. We sat at my scratched-up kitchen table while Brad hooked up the oxygen tank.

"You're aware, Gray, that there's no smoking allowed around this machine," said Brad. "And no candles. This here's pure oxygen and extremely flammable. It'll take out this whole dome."

"Oh, okay." Shit, I didn't know. I looked around at my candles. "I guess we'll just use flashlights at night then."

Brad went outside to get an extension cord.

"But you probably won't need the machine out here. I mean, just take a deep breath."

She did and immediately started to cough.

"Well, maybe I should open the windows. But it's pretty hot out and having them shut keeps it cooler." I waved my arms around. "So what do you think?"

Maggie smiled. "It's cool. Geodesic. That means an open framework of polygons." She took a deep breath. "It combines a sphere with a tetrahedron."

I laughed. "Whatever."

"Oh, I meant to tell you," she said, taking another noisy breath. "Davis called to say he couldn't make it out this week. His dad grounded him after school. He didn't say why. And some girl called. She had a strange name like Seal…"

"Ciel?"

"Yeah. I told her you'd be back next Saturday. She asked me how I was doing. She sounded nice."

Oh, yeah. She wants me.

"So, let's set you up with your computer and the bed. We have drinking water out of the sink tap but no real indoor plumbing. So I set up, behind that curtain," I pointed, "a kind of uh… toilet, that you can use if you're not up to walking to the outhouse. Or say you have to go in the middle of the night. I'll just empty it every morning."

"Gross," said Maggie.

"I know but, hey, it's cave living."

"Pretty fancy cave."

"Yeah, pretty amazing, huh? I couldn't believe when that truck showed up. Isn't this floor cool?"

She nodded and her breath seemed to catch and she struggled for air. I felt myself tense. Brad came in the door.

"You need to hook up to this?" he asked her, holding up the oxygen tube.

* * *

Nacie brought us extra food and lent us more pillows so Maggie could sit propped up in bed and see the view. Mr. D. even banged together a little lap table that straddled her legs so she could do her school work on her computer. He let me off work. Said I should spend these few days with my sister.

The first day I piggy-backed her down to the pond and we had lunch under the weeping willow, fed the ducks bits of bread. When we tried to check on the duck nest, we were chased away by an angry mother duck. We hunted chicken eggs instead, so I could make her my famous omelet. I warned her to watch out for Clarence but he didn't come around. As if he could sense she was sick and off-limits. I was beginning to think he was pretty smart for a dumb bird.

I caught one of the monster bullfrogs for Maggie and took a picture with the ugly butt squatting on her head. I took pictures of her feeding a deer cherries out of her hand. Another of her at dusk, standing under a swarm of bats. We watched the sun set, the clouds all crazy pink and lavender. I'd learned that the more pollution there was in the air, the more dramatic the sunset colors, but I didn't tell Mag that.

After the sun went down, we counted frog croaks. She got tired pretty early and I read to her from Harry Potter. Reading to Maggie was something Mom had started doing, since Maggie's eyes often ached late in the day. I wasn't a big reader but got into the story.

I had a hard time sleeping what with the noise of the oxygen machine. I wasn't used to sleeping in the same room with someone, and every little move of hers woke me up. Not to mention I was camped on the floor.

Maggie couldn't go very long without her oxygen. Said she was needing to use it even more than at home for some reason. Luckily it was sunny every day, so the generator kept it going no problem. But I didn't get it.

"Probably just because I'm excited being here," she said.

By the third day, though, I couldn't even take her down to the pond because she needed to stay on the oxygen. Her breathing had tightened right up and was now a constant wheeze.

On the last night, I made her a meal of lamb chops, mashed potatoes and fresh garden peas with Nacie's brownies for dessert. But Maggie said she wasn't very hungry and had only a tiny taste of a brownie.

"Do you think Mom and Dad are going to break up?" she asked, boom, out of nowhere.

"Man, I don't know. They're just stressed is all. Once this is over… I mean, once you're better, they'll chill out and be fine."

"Don't be mad at Dad."

"Well, I'm surprised you're not mad at him – "

"It's a male thing," she said. "I read about it in *National Geographic*. Male brains process emotions differently. He's just really sad."

"I guess." I was a guy, and I wasn't being an asshole.

"When I die, they'll need you to come home."

"First of all, you're going to get better," I said, clearing the table because I had to do something. "And second of all, I don't know if I'll ever come home. It would be like a backwards step."

Maggie had a coughing attack despite being hooked up to oxygen. It took awhile for her to calm down. I helped her into bed after that and then did the dishes. She was so tired she didn't even want to be read to.

The next morning, Maggie didn't look so good, so I was kind of glad Dad was picking her up. I figured she needed new meds. She'd barely touched her breakfast –

Nacie's oatmeal bread and homemade cherry jam – when I noticed Dad's car turning off the main road.

"Dad's here," I told Maggie and high-tailed it down to introduce him to the D.s. Nacie was there first and did the introductions herself. Mr. D. was "hunting firewood," as she put it.

I directed Dad to drive the car up the hill.

"Just head for the Earth Friendly sign."

"Can't miss it," said Nacie.

"Saw it a good mile down the road," said Dad.

I refused his offer of a ride up the hill and jogged behind him instead. I hadn't been in a car for two months now and wasn't about to start.

"How's Maggie?" he asked, closing the car door.

I was hoping for some sort of comment about the dome. Or the two solar panels positioned on the ground in front of it. Those solar panels, I'd found out, cost twelve hundred apiece. I mean, he had to be impressed.

"How's her energy?" he asked.

"Her energy's a little low. Worn out by the excitement of being out here. Of cave-living," I said with a little laugh. "I thought her breathing would be a lot better out here but…"

Dad stopped listening and went inside the dome.

"Hi, Dad," wheezed Maggie from the bed, barely lifting her hand hello.

"I made the bed with my own hands," I said as he bent down beside Maggie and felt her head. "And the side table, too."

"You feel warm?" he asked her, ignoring me.

"A little." She coughed.

"What's that smell?" asked Dad, finally looking around the place a little.

He walked over to feel the dome material, tap on the windows.

"Pretty cool, eh?" I said, ready to point out all the features.

"The air is terrible in here, Gray. This polyester material doesn't breathe, and it would be newly fireproofed with polybromid diphenyl ethers, and these vinyl windows aren't much better. New material, as you know, off-gasses the most intensely. I thought you said it was made of natural stuff."

"I thought that smell was... well, I didn't think. Sorry, I just assumed since it was – "

"Not only are you living in some toxic bubble, but you're a front man for it." He picked up Maggie in his arms.

"I'm sorry. I should have – "

"Grab her bag and laptop, please," said Dad. "We've got to get you home, Maggie."

Man, how could I be so stupid? I picked up Maggie's things and followed. I wanted to defend myself somehow but couldn't think how.

As we stepped out of the dome, who should be standing there but Cynthia from that TV station, Greg the camera-head beside her, zooming in on me. Judging by the excitement in her hungry face, she had overheard the conversation.

"So it's true, Gray, that you've sold out to Solar Industries?"

* * *

Dad and Maggie had left. And since I refused to answer
any of Cynthia's questions — which was probably just as
incriminating as answering them — she finally left, too.

I was sitting on my stump, thinking things couldn't get
any worse when Mr. D. came up behind me carrying an
armload of weeds.

"Hi, Mr. D." I was trying to sound cheerful. "I'm ready
to work. Was just saying good-bye to my – "

"I don't want you here anymore," he said. "You've
deceived me and my wife as well as your good family."
Beside him Litze gave a low growl.

"Pardon me?"

He shook the greenery in his hands.

Oh, shit. Davis's girls.

"Are these yours?"

"Well…" I wanted to say they were only half mine.

"Answer me."

"Yes."

He looked so disappointed and so hurt, I felt like crap.

"I will keep this between you and me but, young man,
you should be ashamed of yourself for using us in this
way." Litze growled again and bared her teeth. She was
definitely not smiling.

"I understand," I said, feeling more ashamed than he
could know. "I'm really sorry. It was totally stupid and
thoughtless of me."

"You take these straight to the compost bin and dig
them in deep so Nacie doesn't see them."

"Yes, sir."

"Then start packing. You need to go home to your family. Being with them at a time like this is a thousand times more important than this publicity stunt of yours."

He was right. I wasn't helping Maggie. I was running away from her. Because Maggie, I suddenly knew as sure as I knew my own name, was not going to get better.

22 An Open Window

I arrived home on Saturday, tail between my legs. As I stepped inside the house, I saw more letters addressed to me on the table in the hall.

Those were going to stop real soon — in fact, as soon as people tuned into the six o'clock news. "Poster Boy Sells Out," would be the headline. Or "Nature Boy Goes Commercial."

The only letter I'd be writing was to Mr. D. and Nacie. Thanking them for taking me in and apologizing to Nacie for leaving so abruptly. I had to be with my sister, I'd tell her. Which was true.

Dad was coming down the stairs, a tray in his hand.

"Home for the weekend?" he said.

"No. Home for good," I smiled weakly. "Thought I should help you out. And be with Maggie. I really am sorry I was… so stupid about that dome that I didn't realize — "

"No worries. We've all made mistakes here." He looked me right in the eye, gave me a sad but warm smile. "I'm glad you're back."

I felt like crying suddenly, like some lame little kid. I forced the feeling down.

"How is she?"

His smile dissolved. "Her pain level seems to have made a dramatic leap. I don't know if the tumors have all grown that one centimeter more to press on various nerves or what. I've upped her pain medication. So, well, she's more tired. And her feet and ankles are swollen. I was actually just going to call the doctor to find out what that might mean."

"Can I see her?"

"Sure." He continued past me to the kitchen, then stopped. "She had a really good time at the farm. Told me all about it. I'm glad you two spent the time together."

Me, too, I wanted to say, but I couldn't get the words out because my throat had closed right up, my eyes pricking again.

I knocked and went in. She was lying in bed, her face an off color, her breathing even more strained than before.

Though her eyes looked to be closed, she smiled and said, "Gray."

"Yeah, it's me."

She opened her eyes. "You look sad," she wheezed.

"Lost my job." I wanted to tell her the truth.

"How come?"

"Mr. D. found Davis's dope plants up in the woods."

"Graydumb," she said, shaking her head.

"That's me."

* * *

Dad and I took turns waiting on Maggie who, though kind of dopey on medication, was in okay spirits. Dad and I got along all right. It was like we'd forgotten about all the crap that went down over the past few months and just focused on Maggie.

I took over the recycling and composting. Even dug up the garden. I'd gotten used to physical work and my muscles were itching to do stuff. Dad let me put up a laundry line since I offered to hang out wet clothes so we didn't use the dryer. And together he and I cleaned up Mom's studio. At night we watched TSN together, talked about baseball stats or some hockey trade.

Dad called Grammy and Aunt Judy every day to get an update on Mom. I didn't realize how bad off she was. Apparently she was as drugged up as Maggie, only for a different kind of pain. I only wished I could take back what I said.

I slept upstairs in the guest room – my old room – because it shared a wall with Maggie's room and I'd be able to hear if she rang the emergency bell Dad had put beside her bed.

I touched in with Davis and told him about the tragic end of his girls. He was pretty bummed but then made a bad joke about it in the next breath. "Chuck Norris doesn't smoke weed. He gets high roundhouse kicking the THC out of it."

I was hoping I'd hear from Ciel again. Maybe she'd seen the news and decided she'd been right all along. I was a loser. And because I was a prick to her on the phone that time, I couldn't blame her.

* * *

"Take your picture?" I said, hauling out my camera. I'd just helped Maggie to the bathroom and then back to bed.

I aimed the camera and she stuck out her tongue. It was a darkish red with pale white dots along its edge. It looked like a strawberry. Even after brushing, her breath was foul these days, but I didn't say anything.

I took her picture. She posed again, making bunny ears over her head.

Looking at Maggie through my camera lens, I suddenly felt all the tension in my muscles let go. That restless edge of wanting to hurry life along, make it different, better, brighter… to be cooler, smarter and more dope than the next guy was gone. I'd never felt so relaxed yet at the same time so alert and clear-headed.

"Hurry up, Gray," said Maggie. "My arm's tired."

The feeling disappeared and I took her picture.

That night, as I lay in bed listening for sounds from Maggie's room, I tried to recapture the feelings. But it wasn't something I could just make happen.

What the hell did it mean, anyway?

I rolled over, tugged the covers up over my shoulder, and Maggie's G_2L popped to mind.

That was it, I thought. That was what it felt like. Two parts gratitude and one part love.

* * *

I'd been home for nearly two weeks. Mom was due home in two days. She was doing much better, Grammy said when we called. It was the first time we got to talk to her, including Dad. He took the phone in the other room to talk in private, and came back out all nervous looking as he passed me the phone. I was nervous, too.

"Hey, Mom. How are you feeling?"

She said she was better and getting some much-needed rest.

I hardly recognized her voice, it was so shaky, like an old person's.

"Grammy and Aunt Judy have been spoiling me rotten. Won't let me lift a finger around here. But I hear you've come home. I'm so so glad, Gray." She sounded like she might cry, so I quickly told her that I'd been sleeping upstairs in my old room and that Grammy and Aunt Judy could have my suite when they came. "I've changed the sheets and cleaned the bathroom and stuff."

"Okay, that sounds good. Thanks for looking after that."

Grammy and Aunt Judy were flying back with Mom to help out. I was relieved to hear it and looking forward to seeing them. Aunt Judy was really upbeat and funny. Grammy was big into manners and pretty bossy but we could probably use her right about now.

Mom wanted to talk to Maggie so I took the phone upstairs and stayed outside in the hall long enough to hear Maggie say in an unusually strong voice, "I'm feeling fine. Dad and Gray are doing everything perfect. You don't have to worry at all. I've missed you, too. I love you, too, Mom." Then she added, "Don't be sad." She said it like it was an order. "It's going to be all right."

* * *

That afternoon, after hanging out some laundry, I was lying on the bed beside Maggie. Dad was out shopping and filling her prescriptions. She'd been going through the pain pills pretty good.

I had just taken a few "artistic" shots of her. Had arranged her troll collection, about twenty-five in all, in circles around her head so she looked like some freakish flower person. I was feeling creative and she didn't seem to mind. I had her frown, looked scared, surprised, etc. I think they came out pretty good.

Now her head rested heavy against my shoulder. The oxygen box roared in the corner and, as usual, I had to be careful not to lie on the tubing. I was reading aloud her science-nerd mag, some article about creatures that live out their lives encased in ice floes in the Antarctic. Maggie, her voice a raspy whisper, was asking a bunch of science-nerd questions that I couldn't answer, like, "What do they eat?" "How do they keep from freezing themselves?" "Can they mate in ice?"

I was almost finished the article when she grabbed my arm with the kind of strength I didn't think she had left in her any more. Her eyes were wide with what looked like surprise, her mouth open.

"I can't see," she said. There was awe in her voice.

"You can't see?"

Her eyes looked perfectly normal. She was staring straight ahead. Seeing nothing? Only blackness?

"White," she whispered, as if she was reading my mind. It was a spooky moment.

"Should I call Dad? Or maybe an ambulance?" My adrenaline had kicked in and I was trying not to panic.

"No," she said so soft and sure that I didn't move or say anything more. Her hand tightened on my arm like she wanted to keep me there, keep me with her.

Then she touched an ear.

"You can't hear?" I asked. She didn't respond.

I recalled something from biology class on aging and death. Mrs. Kaliba had said that the senses of the dying person leave them one by one. The crudest ones first, the subtler ones last. Smell, she said, was supposed to be the last.

I watched Maggie there beside me. She seemed alert, watchful, her lips slightly parted. Together we waited, my heart beating hard enough for us both.

When her hand loosened its grip on my arm, I slipped my arm around her shoulders to hold onto her. Which was a little different than holding her. I stroked her head where it lay on her pillow.

"I'm here. It's all right, Mag," I mumbled, not believing a word of it.

I should call 911, I told myself. But somehow there wasn't time, wasn't room. The only right thing to do, it seemed, was to focus on Maggie.

"Just relax," I said, talking more to myself. I watched her blind eyes slowly close, a permanent kind of shutting. Holy shit.

"Maggie?" I said and held on tighter. "Open your eyes." My breath was now louder than the oxygen box.

Then I felt a shudder go through her body. It seemed

to start from her legs and continued up to her head, as if something was trying to shake itself free. A second later, a puff of stinky air rushed past her lips and her hand slipped from my arm. Her body seemed to deflate down into my side.

No. No way! I had an overwhelming urge to jump up and get away from her. From it. But I was more afraid of disturbing. The surreally relaxed weight of her body contrasted my own, which was frozen. Life, I realized, is not physically relaxing. Death, on the other hand…

My heart lurched around in my chest. Was she really dead? She was just here a minute ago. We were just here. Could it just happen, like that?

I wanted to snap my fingers. Snap us both out of this weird dream. It was the middle of the day, after all. People didn't die at two in the afternoon. Not on a Saturday.

I gently tugged the oxygen tubes from her nose and put my hand under her nostrils. Then up to her mouth. I stared down at her chest, fooling my eyes into thinking that I saw it lift and fall. Even with the warmth of her body against mine, I felt cold.

After I don't know how long, I eased myself out from under her and gently laid her head back on the pillow. I put my ear against her chest. Nada. Then I stood on what felt like truly hollow legs and looked down at her.

I was thankful her eyes were closed. And no blood. The muscles of her face were so slack, I now saw the outline of several small tumors under the skin on either side of her nose, more along her jawline.

Her body was perfectly still, yet the air all around me felt charged. I was freaked to think that Maggie's consciousness, her "soul music," was unleashed in this very room. Maybe I'd seen too many horror flicks, but a part of me waited for things to start flying around the room.

I took several loud, deep breaths and had to admit that the feeling in the air wasn't scary or bad at all. In fact, it felt all right. It felt like Maggie.

Suddenly I remembered what she'd asked me, the thing about opening a window. Hoping my timing wasn't way off here, I quickly went and opened one. A wet breeze billowed the silkscreen curtains. It was raining lightly, a warm rain.

"Okay, Maggie," I whispered. "Off you go."

Maybe I should have been frantically making phone calls. But I didn't want to. I didn't think Maggie wanted me to, either. I waited, watching the wind whip her curtains around and the rain leave shimmery dots on the wood floor.

Outside, the clouds shifted so that the afternoon sun hit Maggie's upper body, her skin as pale as her silky white pajamas, La Senza Girl written in hot pink across the breast pocket. The light made her look transparent, like an empty chrysalis, as if she really had taken leave of her skin.

My camera was there on her dresser. I picked it up and took several quick pictures before the clouds shifted and the light changed.

Death wasn't what I'd call pretty, but it wasn't ugly, either. It was just what it was. But the thing that was most clear to me after taking those pictures was that this human form was definitely not Maggie anymore.

I don't how long it had been since what they call the time of death – maybe fifteen minutes, maybe more – before I called Dad on his cell.

"Gray, what is it?"

"It's Maggie." I said this slowly, calmly, because, well, the time for panicking had passed.

No response. I meant to say the words, but they wouldn't form in my mouth. Maybe he knew by the tone of my voice.

"I'm coming," he said and quickly hung up.

As I waited for him to arrive, I forced myself to sit in Maggie's room. It didn't feel right to leave her body alone. Even though she may have escaped out that window.

I placed a chair beside the bed and I held her hand, which now felt weirdly heavy, cold, too.

But I held on.

23 Endings and Their Opposite

We didn't do any big funeral thing. Maggie's body – her shell, as I thought of it – we simply cremated and the ashes were returned to us in a silver urn. What we did have instead was a big party. A wake, was what Grammy called it. "A celebration of Maggie's life."

She and Aunt Judy did the cooking, Dad and I the cleaning. We weren't going to bother Mom, who spent her days painting a mural on Maggie's wall. That's what she wanted to do so we let her. "Her catharsis," Grammy called it.

Having more or less gotten through the benzene guilt thing, Mom was messed up all over again for not having been with Maggie at the end. For not being able to say good-bye. There was a part of me that believed Maggie wanted it that way, but I didn't know how to say that without it coming out wrong.

Whenever Mom started in on her broken-record guilt routine, Grammy was usually the one who talked her out of it and back into the present moment. While she did this, Aunt Judy would quickly massage Mom's shoulders. But the morning of the party, it was just Mom and I in the kitchen because Dad had driven Aunt Judy to the store for some candles, and Grammy was in the shower.

Mom was talking fast, shaking her head, her eyes looking all scary and distant like that day I mentioned the benzene.

"If only I hadn't gone away. I could have stayed and – "

"I have pictures," I blurted, and Mom stopped talking. "Lots of them, from when Maggie first got sick up until the day she died. Maybe… you'd… would you like to see Maggie?"

Mom focused her eyes on me. Nodded her head.

"Yes, Gray, I would."

"Great. I'll get my laptop. You make some tea, okay?"

"Okay."

Grammy was just coming out of the bathroom. I told her what had happened.

"Do you think it's all right to show her pictures of Maggie?"

"I think that'll be good, Gray. I'll be right along."

As I was setting my laptop up on the kitchen table, Dad and Aunt Judy arrived.

"Just in time for the slide show," I said, glancing sideways at Mom, who was fidgeting with her hands.

I'd made the pictures large enough to fill the screen, and when Maggie's smiling face appeared, Mom gasped, tears springing to her eyes.

My eyes darted to Grammy.

She nodded at me that it was okay.

"There's your beautiful girl, Julia and Ethan," she said

in a soothing voice. "She had a wonderful life because of you two. Not to mention her wonderful brother."

Aunt Judy moved to do the massage thing, but Dad was already there. Very gently, he placed his hands on Mom's shoulders. Mom's eyes closed for a moment and my stomach clenched, waiting for her reaction. It was the first time I'd seen them touch in a long time.

Without looking at him, she placed her hand over his. My gut instantly relaxed and then I felt ridiculously happy inside.

I clicked up the next picture: Maggie examining a jar of rice. Then another of her wagging a finger as she talked to it. I didn't explain the pictures and nobody asked me to. Still touching Dad's hand, Mom started crying softly. Grammy nodded for me to go on.

There were pictures of Maggie sleeping with her mouth slung open, another of her pigging out on that Blizzard. There were pictures of her with her friends and some of her with Davis, who looked retarded. I'd ordered the pictures chronologically and I noticed now how her skin got more pale, the circles under her eyes darker, her body more shrunken. It was like watching a speeded-up version of her dying. Yet the spirit in her eyes never changed and I hoped everyone could see that, too.

Then came the pictures I'd taken of her on the farm — against the backdrop of the brilliant sunset, of her lifting two eggs from its grassy nest and some of her feeding that deer. There were others by the pond and then one with that bullfrog on her head.

"Is that a frog on her head?" asked Mom, who had stopped crying and was leaning in for a closer look.

"Yeah," I said.

Then came the pictures of Maggie with trolls around her head. In the first one she wore this big dumb smile and the whole thing looked totally demented.

Suddenly Mom barked out a laugh, startling us. Dad started to laugh, too. By the time I clicked through the rest of the troll head pics, we were all laughing our heads off

But I knew what was next. The dead shots. I didn't want to show them. But I felt I had to.

I waited until the laughter had faded, held my breath and clicked up the first one.

And it was okay.

* * *

Tons of people came to the party. All of Maggie's teachers from kindergarten on, which meant a lot of my old teachers and it was seriously awkward talking to some of them. Maggie's friends came all red-eyed because they'd had a group cry outside first. Neighbors whose names we didn't even know showed up with casseroles, pots of chili, loaves of banana bread. There were all of Dad's friends and people from the university. Mom's friends and various clients, even a woman from the bank. The Daskaloffs showed up, too, Nacie bringing a platter of brownies big enough to feed a small country. When Mr. D. saw me, he came straight over and put his arm around my shoulder.

"You're a good boy," he told me and gave me a squeeze. I'd lost most of the muscle I'd gained during my time as a farmhand. I thought he was going to pop my shoulder out of place.

Davis was there and, being a big mushball, was the most teary-eyed person at the whole party. Hughie and Parm came by, and even Nat and her gang. They just stayed long enough to say they were sorry about Maggie and to nab some brownies, but it was good to see them.

Hughie confessed he felt all messed up about the last time he saw Maggie.

"Shit, Gray, I mooned her. That was the last thing I ever got to say to her. Here's my ass."

"Means you're going straight to hell when it's your last party," said Davis, his mouth full of brownie.

Chrissy asked if I was coming back to school in the fall.

"Yeah, I'm back. Thinking of joining the E-Club."

They all stopped and looked at me to see, I think, if I was joking. When it was obvious I wasn't, Hughie said, "That's cool."

I'd been talking to Dad about the environmental studies program at the university, which sounded really cool. But in memory of Maggie, and to keep the balance, I'd be having myself a Blizzard every so often, too.

By now I'd shaken way too many hands and listened to way too many people saying how sorry they were, so Davis and I piled a plate full of watermelon and brownies and escaped downstairs to sit outside by the hot tub.

It was perfect weather, sunny and warm. We had a watermelon-seed spitting contest. Though I was trying damn hard, Davis always shot his the farthest.

Then I flashed on Maggie's G_2L thing and stopped trying so hard. I relaxed my mouth, just appreciated that seed in my mouth and how my cheek and lip muscles worked together with my tongue to simply… spit.

"Hey, I beat you," I said.

Even Davis looked surprised.

"You win," he said, "and I got to take a piss. I drank way too much punch." He got up and headed inside. "Don't eat all the brownies."

I leaned back in my chair, lifted my face to the sun and closed my eyes. I wondered if wherever Maggie was now, there was such a thing as warm and cold.

I felt a shadow block my sun, and I opened my eyes.

"Ciel," I blurted and sat up real quick. There she was, like magic, just standing beside my chair. I hadn't heard a thing.

"Hi, Gray. Sorry, I didn't mean to disturb…"

I don't know what got into me – some of Maggie's fearlessness, maybe – but hearing that musical voice ripped me out of my chair. I stepped right up to her and looked into her eyes. She stopped talking and I hugged her. Because she was right in front of me, alive and warm, and I didn't want to miss the chance.

She felt so good to hold. And when I felt her hold me back, my eyes closed.

I opened them to see Davis's lips and nose smashed up against the window of the door as he kissed it. I laughed out loud and hugged Ciel harder.

* * *

The next day Mom, Dad and I scattered Maggie's ashes in the creek in the park up behind the D.s' farm. It was my idea. I thought Maggie'd appreciate that her ashes, like her soul, were going on an adventure, a journey.

The large gray flakes floated on the water's surface, and we watched as they swept downhill toward the sea.

Maybe some would end up clinging to the creek shore and becoming part of the soil. Maybe some would nourish a fish or two, others mixing in with the water and becoming part of the cycle of evaporation. Then Maggie would be part of the clouds and the rain, too.

And when that Maggie rain fell in a cold place, she would freeze into so many seriously dope crystals.